HARD HAND
TITANS: SIN CITY

SIERRA CARTWRIGHT

HARD HAND

Copyright @ 2018 Sierra Cartwright

First E-book Publication: July 2018

Editor: Nicki Richards, What's Your Story Editorial Services

Line Editing by Jennifer Barker

Proofing by Bev Albin, ELF

Layout Design by Riane Holt

Cover Design by Once Upon An Alpha

Photographer: Annie Ray at Passion Pages

Cover Model: Justin Edwards

Photo provided by @Annie Ray/Passion Pages

Promotion by Once Upon An Alpha, Shannon Hunt

All rights reserved. Except for use in a review, no part of this publication may be reproduced, distributed, or transmitted in any form, or by any means, electronic or mechanical, including photocopying, recording, or by any information storage and retrieval system, without prior written permission of the author.

This is a work of fiction. Names, characters, places, brands, media, and incidents are either the products of the author's imagination or are used fictitiously, and any resemblance to any actual persons, living or dead, is entirely coincidental.

The author acknowledges the trademarked status and trademark owners of various products referenced in this work of fiction. The publication/use of these trademarks is not authorized, associated with, or sponsored by the trademark owners.

Adult Reading Material

Disclaimer: This work of fiction is for mature (18+) audiences only and contains strong sexual content and situations.

It is a standalone with my guarantee of satisfying happily ever after.

All rights reserved.

DEDICATION

For Angel Payne, Victoria Blue, and Miss Whit...and one afternoon in Dallas that led to a magic collaboration and this story. Thanks also to Mari Carr, Red Phoenix, Jenna Jacob, Shannon Hunt, and Lorraine Gibson for the support in bringing the project to life!

Thanks also to Kierstin, ELF, Bad Ass Bev, my ARC team, beta readers, and the fabulous members of my reader group, Sierra's Super Stars.

More than ever, I know that producing a book takes a team. I'm grateful to be surrounded by wonderful people. Thank you!

CHAPTER ONE

*C**ole Stewart.*
Breathing in jagged hiccups, Avery glanced again at the tuxedoed gentleman. No one else was that tall and imposing, hardened by numerous tours of duty overseas, and —if rumors were correct—some sort of undercover work. He moved his head to study the stage, and the light caught the scar on his cheek. The jagged white line arrowed downward, ending dangerously close to his jugular. Her last doubt vanished. It was definitely Cole Stewart.

She curled her toes in her too-high, too-expensive designer sandals. *What is he doing here?* She'd been over the guest list for her great-aunt's eightieth birthday extravaganza dozens of times. The Sensational Miss Scarlet had been a mainstay in Las Vegas for more than six decades and had made hundreds of friends. Because she wanted everyone she cared about to attend her Saints and Sinners masquerade ball, the names of the invitees had been studied and restudied for more than a year.

A man wearing a security guard uniform emblazoned

with the Royal Sterling Hotel's logo, entered the room and stood next to Cole.

Since Avery was behind the elaborate champagne fountain wearing a fabulous ornate black mask, she was free to feast her gaze on Cole, the Dominant of her fantasies.

His dark hair was longer than she remembered. It was no longer tortured by a military buzz. Instead, strands teased the collar of his jacket. The look didn't tame him. It simply made him more roguish.

Although Cole wasn't classically handsome, he was rugged in a don't-fuck-with-me kind of way. His physique was more sumptuous than ever. Everything about him from his size to his stance promised he was capable of protecting his woman. And she knew he could make one scream from pleasure.

A memory of watching him interact with a submissive lanced through Avery, and she squirmed.

Two years prior, she'd been at a BDSM play party at the home of her friends and renowned legal eagles, Diana and Alcott Hewitt. Cole had entered with his submissive, Gia. Most times when Avery watched scenes, the partners appeared to be in sync, maybe a little in love. But Gia had goaded him. In addition to addressing him disrespectfully, she chose to ignore some of his commands. He never raised his voice or lost his temper. Instead, he'd continued to state his wishes without emotion. Gia had responded, however, to his gentle caresses.

Once he'd taken her down from the Saint Andrew's cross, he was tender, and Gia leaned into him.

Avery longed to be with a man as patient and firm as Cole.

Many times, she masturbated to thoughts of him. Once, when she'd been with another man, she pretended she was with Cole.

About six months ago, she'd seen him again at the Back Room, an upscale BDSM club. This time he was alone. He kept to himself, brooding, detached.

She'd been alone for year, and she craved a hard hand to soothe her. But the breakup with her Dominant had left her emotionally uncertain. As she watched Cole across the dungeon, she mentally rehearsed and discarded a dozen openings. Walk up to him and kneel? Meet him as an equal? Ask mutual friends for an introduction? Hope he would notice her interest?

After more than an hour of indecision, she convinced herself to say hello. But the moment she'd gotten close to him and their gazes met, she froze. Even though she was an experienced BDSM player, she'd never had a visceral reaction like she did to Cole. His eyes—charcoal and intense—pierced her submissive soul. Nerves trumped courage. She started to tremble. In the end, she couldn't force herself to take the final steps.

Ever since, she regretted that night, and she'd vowed to be braver if given a second chance.

Now that she was in the same room as him again, she understood her own cowardice. With his arms folded across his chest, legs braced apart, he was a force of nature.

Perhaps sensing scrutiny, he turned in her direction, and his powerful gaze locked on her. He scanned her body, starting at her shoes and sweeping up. Cole took so much time that her internal temperature spiked. When he reached her face, he quirked an eyebrow, as if in recognition. *That's not possible*. They'd never met, never spoken. Even if they had, she was still hidden behind a mask, and she'd traded in her long light-brown hair for shoulder-length blonde with bright-pink streaks.

Still, just like that night, she trembled.

Marie, the party planner, strode through a side door.

Electronic pad clutched in her hands, she made a direct line to where Avery stood. "Does everything look all right?"

Grateful to be jolted from the nerve-wrecking memories, Avery replied, "It's perfect." And it was. The stage was set in a retro manner, including oversize square microphones. The band members wore tuxedos. Several food stations were in place with hors d'oeuvres for the wine hour. Around the periphery of the room, tall tables were draped with black or silver tablecloths and decorated with soaring centerpieces crafted from flowers, masks, and peacock feathers. And there was dazzle everywhere—sequins and crystals strung from the ceilings, tacked to the walls—all befitting one of the country's most accomplished and scandalous burlesque dancers.

Backstage, a number of entertainers wore gold or silver body paint and nothing else. They represented sinners for the evening. Others were dressed in nuns' habits or monks' robes. A couple of women even wore halos.

"Have you tried the champagne?" Marie questioned.

"Not yet. Should I?"

"Please."

From a nearby table, Avery grabbed a flute and held it beneath a stream of the flowing pink bubbly. Of course Miss Scarlet had selected a rosé. It had been a favorite since she saw *An Affair to Remember* with Cary Grant and Deborah Kerr. Miss Scarlet said she'd once shared a glass with Cary himself. Though Avery wasn't sure about that, she didn't doubt it was possible.

She took a small drink, expecting it to be overly sweet. She was surprised by complexity. "Wow. It's fantastic."

"That's what I thought."

Seduced, Avery savored another sip before putting the glass down. "I'm betting this isn't the fifty-dollar-a-bottle stuff that I approved?"

Marie winced. "Miss Scarlet was at the tasting, and when she sampled this stuff…"

"Say no more." Even though Avery served as her great-aunt's financial advisor, Miss Scarlet controlled her own fortune. If she wanted to drop five hundred dollars a pop for the best bubbly on the planet, that was her choice.

"I'm sorry to say we didn't save any money on the dessert either."

Avery sighed. "I'm not surprised."

"You will be," she replied cryptically.

"Oh?" Avery arched her eyebrows.

"Your aunt is planning something extravagant. With a cake. Of sorts."

"You don't think I should have been warned?"

"I promised secrecy." Marie pantomimed locking her lips and tossing away the key. "But I can tell you the changes have thrown us about fifty thousand dollars over budget."

Stunned, Avery blinked. "I assume she knows that?"

"Yes."

"In that case, we should enjoy every moment."

A door closing at the back of the room made her turn around. Cole was gone. She sighed in relief, but then a stab of restlessness went through her. "Were there last-minute additions to the guest list?"

"Not that I know of."

"I saw Cole Stewart a few minutes ago."

"Who?"

The most gorgeous man on the planet. "He's the billionaire security tech genius who sold his first company to Julien Bonds." According to an article in *Scandalicious,* her favorite online gossip site, Cole's groundbreaking software package was now installed on every new Bonds device.

Marie typed the name into her pad.

"He was talking to someone I assume was with security."

Marie shook her head. "He's not on the list. No one will get in without an invitation. I'll chat with Lucy and see what's up."

"Thank you."

Lucy Pine was the Royal Sterling's head of security. The petite woman might reach five feet tall in her heeled boots, but she was badass enough to take down the hardest of criminals, all without her braid coming undone.

"Anything else?" Marie asked.

"You've done a great job. I'll go check on my aunt."

"The doors will open in about twenty minutes. Make it quick?" Marie pleaded.

"Promise." Avery headed toward the elevator that had access to the building's top floors.

Maybe because of the alcohol or her stupid-high heels—but definitely not because of Cole Stewart—she had to steady herself on a railing when the car rocketed past the spa level, then the hotel floors.

With a soft *ding*, the car arrived, and she exited into a gorgeous long hallway. She made her way to her great-aunt's condominium that had an awe-inspiring view of the Strip. Miss Scarlet said she loved lording over Las Vegas. Over the years, she'd seen a lot of changes and mostly liked them. At times, though, she sighed wistfully, still missing a particular dark and dangerous mobster she'd had a mad affair with.

Avery knocked on her great-aunt's door, and the summons was answered by none other than Mademoiselle Giselle, a New Orleans shop owner and ballerina of international renown.

"I had to see Miss Scarlet in her outfit," the woman admitted after accepting Avery's gentle embrace. "We've got a busy night, but I couldn't resist bringing her some flowers."

There were at least a dozen more bouquets than there had been earlier this afternoon. "Are you dancing tonight?"

"Oui. It's my honor."

Mademoiselle and Miss Scarlet had been friends for at least half a century and shared secrets that would only be revealed in a posthumous memoir.

Once Mademoiselle said goodbye, Avery made her way to the living room.

Miss Scarlet was standing on a platform where a seamstress was making final alterations to her costume. A headdress sat off to the side, waiting to be affixed.

Even at eighty, she was a bombshell, with a radiant smile, a fit body, and long legs shown off by slits that ran up the sides of her skirt, almost to her buttocks. A number of feathers had been applied in strategic locations, and a pair of long black gloves were draped over the cheval mirror.

As she'd done almost every night for decades, Miss Scarlet had applied false eyelashes and glittery stage makeup. She completed her ensemble with an artistically placed beauty mark.

Avery leaned in to kiss her great-aunt on the cheek. "Happy birthday."

"I never get tired of hearing that! In fact, I think I should have two birthdays a year now. I love the attention." She batted her eyes. "And the gifts."

Avery grinned.

"Move over there, into the light where I can see you," Scarlet ordered.

Though Avery shook her head from mild embarrassment, she did as she was told. She spun around then offered a little curtsy.

"Bravo! As I imagined, your dress is perfect, and you are magnificent."

Avery struggled with the compliment. When she opened the gift from Miss Scarlet, Avery had stared in shock. She'd never seen anything like the gorgeous clingy black gown. It was cut asymmetrically across her chest and had only one strap. The open back plunged to the base of her spine, leaving her exposed. Since the dress was tighter than most of her clothing, she'd promised herself that she would lose five pounds before the event. Those plans were dashed when the Royal Sterling installed a cupcake-dispensing machine in the hotel's lobby. Willpower had been defeated by a single swipe of her credit card. Still, she was glad she'd worn the dress. It gave her confidence and made her feel sexy.

"Did you try the champagne, darling girl?" In the mirror, Scarlet's gaze found Avery's.

"It's amazing."

"Isn't it? Highly recommended. An online review says it has an evocative finish."

Avery wasn't quite sure what that meant. "I'll take your word for it."

"Don't worry about the budget."

"Aunt Scarlet, it's your money. You should spend it on anything you want."

"That's not what I meant at all." She waved a hand. "I'm going to get Rafe Sterling to pay for it."

"Are you?" Avery had met the CEO of Sterling Worldwide on a couple of occasions. Though he was an excellent businessman, he wasn't involved in the day-to-day operations of each property. "How are you going to manage that?"

"I pack this hotel every night that I perform. And I'm sure he'd like me to sign another contract. All part of the negotiation strategy, my dear." Miss Scarlet winked, and her eyelash twinkled from the glitter dabbed on it. "I won't squander your inheritance on rosé, no matter how good it is."

"You've worked hard every day of your life." The familiar refrain made Avery sigh. "It's you I love, and I want to enjoy your company. That's the only thing that matters."

"Good thing, since I intend to live another forty years."

With no plans of ever retiring. Not only did Miss Scarlet own a studio where she taught dance and exercise classes, she'd recently opened a museum for cabaret memorabilia. Even now, she was choreographing a new burlesque show to debut in the fall.

"Get the party started, will you?" Miss Scarlet suggested. "I'll be down just as soon as I can."

"Marie mentioned a surprise. Anything I should know?"

Miss Scarlet's sculptured eyebrows arched higher. "I've no idea what you're talking about, darling girl."

"That was what I was afraid you'd say." She shook her head. "I saw Cole Stewart downstairs."

"Delicious, isn't he?"

"Is he your guest?"

"He's consulting with hotel security." She hesitated. "He's a…VIP."

"A…" Avery's heart plunged.

"Yes."

Why am I not surprised? Though she was an ordinary person living a very ordinary life, her aunt had found a place in the upper echelons.

Avery had learned about the Zeta Society early on when she'd picked up an owl from her great-aunt's shelf. For years, the statue with its emerald-green eyes had fascinated her, but it wasn't until she was a teenager that Avery questioned its meaning.

Scarlet swore Avery to secrecy about the Zetas—whose members were known as Titans. Politicians belonged, as did royalty, entrepreneurs, writers, Hollywood A-listers, scientists, prize winners in every field, and even members of the Mafia. Initiation fees were astronomical, and yearly dues were equally onerous. Still, the wait list to join was several years long.

"You'll have Marie add his name to the guest list?"

She sighed. "Of course." After giving her great-aunt another quick kiss, she made her way back downstairs. One of the security guards opened the ballroom door for her. She was grateful that Cole wasn't there. Part of her wondered if she'd conjured him from a very vivid imagination. Or maybe an unstated need. It had been forever since she played with a Dom, years since she'd been in a committed relationship.

The banquet captain stood in the middle of a circle of hotel employees, issuing final instructions. Marie was speaking with the head of security, and Avery joined them.

"Marie tells me you were asking about Cole Stewart," Lucy said.

"Miss Scarlet filled me in. Thank you."

"Good. Then it's not a problem if he checks in from time to time?"

Only to my libido. "He's an invited guest."

"Let me know if there's anything you need." With a curt nod, Lucy excused herself.

When they were alone, Marie tapped her electronic pad. "Everything's checked off. Ready?"

"Yes." Avery straightened her mask. "Let's get this party started."

Marie signaled to the band, and they began their instrumental rendition of Frank Sinatra's *Luck Be a Lady* while servers moved into position. A couple of the painted entertainers stood still, appearing to be statues. One perched on the grand piano while another linked arms with a nun in a stunning juxtaposition.

When Marie nodded toward the security guard, he signaled to have the doors opened, and the guests began to file in.

Some headed for the bar, others to turn up chairs and lay claim to tables, and a few made their way toward the food.

For the next thirty minutes, Avery greeted guests while

wondering what was keeping her great-aunt. Part of the surprise?

The moment Cole entered the ballroom, she knew it, even without seeing him.

Wisps of hair rose on her nape as the recognition of his power over her danced down her spine.

Avery desperately wanted to turn and look at him, but she held off, continuing to smile and talk with attendees, pretending an interest she suddenly didn't have.

A tall, thin, gorgeous Black singer stepped onto the stage in a catsuit and started to belt out the words to *Fever*.

Avery watched, entranced as the performer strutted down the stairs to lean against the grand piano. At least a dozen men, snapping their fingers, emerged from behind the curtain to add to the seductive chorus.

She had to admit, Miss Scarlet had done a spectacular job with the music and entertainment selections.

Drawn by the pulse of primal energy in the room, Avery could no longer resist. She glanced over her shoulder to where she instinctively knew Cole was standing.

That familiar spark of fear snaked through her, leaving her rooted to the spot, even though she wanted to go to him.

A waiter passed by, and she snagged a flute. As she sipped, bubbles tickled her nose and heightened her senses. Avery watched the band and performers, trying to shut out thoughts of Cole.

But the harder she tried, the more he occupied her mind.

Every part of her yearned for a Dom. And tonight, not just any Dom. Cole.

So, what am I going to do? The longer she thought about it, the more adrenaline flooded her body, making her jittery.

He could have a girlfriend or submissive at home. Even if he didn't, he could still reject her, but since he wouldn't know who she was, her ego would remain intact.

Since her hand was shaking, she crossed the room to put down her mostly untouched glass.

This was her moment. If she deliberated too long, she might lose her opportunity.

Her stomach dancing with butterflies, she traced the curlicue outline of her mask, drawing courage and reassurance from its anonymity. For tonight, if never again, she wanted to be the woman she was in her dreams.

Avery chatted with some of the guests as she made her way across the room. She smiled until she thought her makeup might crack, all the while keeping an eye on him.

Eventually—too soon and simultaneously not soon enough—she reached him.

For a moment, her words lodged in her throat.

The passage of time had only made him more attractive. The cut of his expensive tailored tuxedo should have made him look civilized. It didn't.

Her nerves doubled.

"Evening." His voice was like the finest liqueur, rich and deep with a hint of sweetness laced through the danger.

Rockets of arousal shot through her. She forced herself to pretend she didn't know who he was and that she wasn't a bundle of apprehension. "Glad to have you at Miss Scarlet's birthday party."

"Cole Stewart."

"A pleasure to meet you. I'm—" She thought for a moment through the onslaught of apprehension. Finally, she seized on a name. "Layla."

He extended his hand, and his ring caught the light. An owl, with inset emeralds for eyes.

Avery slid her palm against his much larger one, and her knees buckled. Instantly, she caught herself, but she was stunned by the strength of her instinct to kneel for him. No doubt, even women who weren't into BDSM would recognize his authority.

"Layla," he echoed with a slight mocking smile, as if he didn't believe her.

He continued to hold her, and his grip was as powerful as she'd expected. It wasn't crushing, however. Cole clearly knew his strength and harnessed it.

"And what do you do?"

"I'm a project accountant for a construction firm. Not very glamorous, but I enjoy it."

"You like having everything neat and tidy?"

"I've never looked at it that way." She shrugged. Even without knowing her, he'd made an accurate guess, not that she was surprised.

"But?"

"You're right. Math is absolute. And I do enjoy chasing down discrepancies so that the numbers add up." How much was he willing to reveal in return? "And you, Mr. Stewart?"

"At the moment, I work as a consultant to Hawkeye Security."

"I've heard of them."

He inclined his head to one side. "Have you?"

"The company I work for has just signed an agreement with them." Curiosity drove her next question. "Are you in Las Vegas permanently?"

"I have a home here, but I don't spend much time in it. As you said about your job, it's not very glamorous. I make recommendations that people don't want to follow." He gave a wry grin, and then the conversation hit a natural lull.

What the hell should she say next? *I can't help but notice how commanding you appear. Are you a Dominant?*

"Which are you?"

Perplexed, she frowned. It was as if he'd read her mind. "I'm sorry?"

"It's a saints or sinners masquerade." He traced a finger around the corner of her mask. For a heart-stopping moment, she thought he might try to take it off her. "I'd say a saint?" He swept his gaze over her. "But in that dress?"

"Ah—"

"There's something innocent about you, but you didn't answer immediately to tell me you were a saint. So that makes me wonder."

This was her chance. He'd offered the opening she hungered for, but her boldness wavered.

Cole leaned forward, indicating his interest in her answer.

Then abruptly, the music ended. Shocked, she turned toward the stage. Whatever was happening wasn't on the program she'd approved a few days ago.

In true gentlemanly form, Cole steadied her by placing his hand on the bare skin of her back. Electricity arced up her spine to settle at her nape. If she had this kind of reaction to his touch, what would it be like to submit?

A spotlight hit the stage, and the band struck up a fun version of *Happy Birthday*.

As she watched with Cole's hand still firmly on her spine, four men in skintight clothing wheeled out a gigantic cake. The thing had numerous layers and a great big candle on the top.

Cole leaned closer, his breath warm on her ear. "Where's Miss Scarlet?"

"No idea," she whispered back.

A chorus line of women in feathers and little else began to sing as the band launched a second run-through of the song.

When they reached the *happy birthday, Miss Scarlet* part, the top of the cake exploded open, and Miss Scarlet emerged.

The crowd cheered. Avery clapped wildly. She should

have suspected her great-aunt would dazzle, but Avery had never guessed she'd make such a stunning entrance.

The song ended, and Miss Scarlet blew kisses as she waved. A hundred cell phones were pulled out, and guests snapped pictures.

Men, in their gold paint, lined up in front of her. Then, in the silence, she dived forward.

Stunned gasps rippled through the guests as she hung suspended in midair, her chin cupped seductively in her palm and her knees bent in a way that made her gown billow about her.

As one, the men undulated, reaching to guide her down, and a spotlight reflected off the silver wire Avery hadn't noticed until now.

As she'd been doing for more than half a century, Miss Scarlet commanded the room while wearing a towering headdress and elaborate costume.

"Isn't she fabulous?" Avery asked Cole.

"She is indeed."

Rather than leaving the stage, Miss Scarlet took a place in front of the chorus line.

A song Avery didn't immediately remember began to play, and a man in a top hat sauntered onto the stage. He stood there, appearing mysterious as a woman strolled in front of him.

Several seconds in, Avery recognized the tune, *I'm a Good Girl*, in which the performer was anything but.

Toward the end of the song, Miss Scarlet was plucked from the stage. In her glittery stilettos, she wrapped herself around the guidewire and made a sensual writhing motion before turning to shake her backside at the crowd.

Several dozen more female cast members exploded onto the scene, wriggling their feathered rears while the male performers raised their eyebrows as well as their top hats.

The full-on burlesque number rocked the room.

Cole said something, and Avery leaned in to hear him.

"She's amazing," he repeated.

"Every day she wows me," Avery confessed.

As the song segued into a new one, a spotlight hit the stage, and a curtain was pulled back. A showstopping rocking horse dominated the scene, at least ten feet tall and ungelded. On his back was a woman dressed in a corset and tulle skirt. As the stallion moved back and forth, the woman undulated her hips provocatively.

Avery watched, shocked and riveted, aware of the way Cole was still touching her and the heat that was flowing through her. It wasn't just from him, but from the raw sex oozing from the cabaret show.

"What do you think?" Cole asked against her ear.

A tremor splashed through her. This was the opening she'd wanted.

Avery turned slightly, grateful she was incognito and could be someone she wasn't, even if it was just for this moment. This time, she prayed courage didn't desert her.

CHAPTER TWO

Cole narrowed his eyes and wondered what the hell game Avery was playing.

No matter how clever she thought she'd been in not using her real name and hiding behind a mask, he would know the beauty anywhere.

Her eyes were wide and luminous, innocent yet provocative. She'd cut her hair, changed from brown to blonde, and added streaks of color.

And none of that mattered.

Her curves were the kind he remembered. His reaction to her was visceral, the same as it had been six months ago when he'd seen her at the Back Room.

He'd thought she might approach him that night. Instead, she vanished.

The next day, he asked mutual friends about her. He learned she was single and that she'd had a bad experience with a Dominant.

This evening, her attempt at casual conversation had charmed him. She'd been seeking out information about his job and where he lived. He didn't need a background as an operative to figure out she was interested in him.

Cole glanced at her ring finger. Bare. But her necklace intrigued him. It was bold, made from interlocking pieces of silver that snuggled against the base of her throat. It didn't appear to be a collar, though it was close enough that he couldn't be certain. Of course, no one who wasn't in the lifestyle would even question the piece of jewelry.

The song ended, and another began, the routine something like the world-famous Rockettes would perform, with high, exciting kicks and energy.

The adorably submissive Avery shifted her weight from one foot to the other, radiating her discomfort. If his guess was correct, she wanted to be on her knees with his hand tangled in her hair, awaiting his command. Right now, if he had a choice, that command would be to suck his cock.

The burlesque show ended, and the performers received a standing ovation.

As the stage was cleared, the band segued into another Frank Sinatra signature song, making it a bit easier to talk. A few couples wandered onto the dance floor, and he had no intention of letting her vanish a second time. "Shall we?" he invited.

Her mouth parted slightly, and he was tempted to kiss away her hesitation.

Where the hell did that thought come from? The tender impulse shocked him. He was not a man given to romance. To distract himself, he held out a hand.

A few seconds later, she accepted.

It was the first step toward dominating her.

On the parquet dance floor, he led to the slow beat, and she followed in flawless moves. Her skin felt luxurious. No matter what he asked for with his body, she responded.

Would she behave the same way in private? Suddenly, he was anxious to get her out of that dress.

The tune ended.

By unspoken accord, they crossed the room to stand near a group of people flocked around Miss Scarlet. She held an open black fan emblazoned with a sequined kitten, and as she spoke, she waved the thing around.

Avery remained close to him, as if they were a couple. It surprised him how much he welcomed that idea.

A waiter passed by with champagne, and Cole asked if she would like one.

"Thank you. No." She shook her head. "I think I've had enough."

"Good." He wanted her sober enough to play with him later. "Tell me about your jewelry," he invited.

"Sorry?"

"Your necklace."

Behind the mask, her eyes widened. She fingered one of the links, probably without being aware of the act.

"Does it have any significance?"

"Something I bought myself recently at an art festival downtown."

"Intriguing," he said.

"How so?"

He was done allowing her to hide. "I wondered if it might indicate an interest in bondage."

"Bondage." She dropped her hand. "Is that something you're into, Mr. Stewart?"

"I generally don't discuss my personal life in a public setting."

"But you're the one who brought it up."

He wondered if she had any idea how breathless her voice was. "So I did. And the answer is yes. Do you know anything about it?"

She was saved from an answer when Miss Scarlet breezed over in a cloud of perfume.

"You were marvelous," Avery enthused.

The woman's smile dazzled, and it encompassed Cole. "You are more handsome every time I see you."

She offered her gloved hand, and he raised it to his lips.

"Always a pleasure, Miss Scarlet. Your entrance was spectacular."

"I do enjoy leaping into the arms of strong young men. I'll be doing that for my ninetieth as well."

"I believe it."

Her attention was claimed by admirers wearing old-fashioned black-and-white-striped prison garb. Sinners, no doubt.

"If you'll excuse me?" Miss Scarlet didn't wait for an answer before flipping open the kitty fan and moving off, leaving him alone again with Avery.

"Where were we?" He figured he'd give her the opportunity to pursue or avoid the question he'd asked her earlier.

"We were talking about bondage." Despite her comment about the necklace not being a collar, she absently touched it again. Then, as if realizing that she was fidgeting, she stilled and lowered her hand. "And yes, I'm familiar with it."

"You're a submissive."

"*What?*"

Cole often worked undercover, and he was skilled at blending in. He could adapt to any environment, appear to be anyone. But a one-on-one relationship was different. After the emotional turmoil left behind when Gia moved out for the third time in a fit of hysteria, he wanted honesty, even if it was uncomfortable and ugly.

For this moment, he'd let her shield her identity, but his tolerance wouldn't last. "You've ascertained I'm a Dom."

"I…" She licked her upper lip.

"Admit it." He leaned in a little closer to her, not enough to intimidate her but enough to let her know that, to him, there were no other people in the room. "Something in you responds to me intuitively, female to male. You won't deny that."

Avery lowered her gaze before shaking her head and looking back up at him.

"What color is your thong?" he asked.

She choked. "Excuse me?"

Avery—*Layla*—lifted a glass of champagne from a passing waiter's tray, but Cole took it from her. "You said you'd had enough. If you'd like this conversation to go any further, you need to drink something nonalcoholic. Your choice."

For a moment, she was contemplative. In her eyes, her struggle played out. She clearly wanted to go forward, and she seemed to be fighting for nerve to say so. When she answered, her voice was barely discernible over the band. "Sparkling water."

"Lime?"

"Yes. Please."

He left her long enough to head to the bar and fetch her a drink. When he returned, she hadn't moved, and she was again tracing the interlocking links on her necklace. He offered her the glass. "I'm waiting for your answer."

"How do you know I'm wearing a thong?"

"No panty lines. And you don't strike me as a woman who would skip her foundation garments unless her Dom told her to." He grinned. "How was my guess?"

She traced the rim of her glass before meeting his gaze. "It's black."

"Lacy." It wasn't a question.

"Yes."

"Take it off."

She blinked.

"You can do it here, or you may excuse yourself to the ladies' room."

"I didn't bring a purse down with me." She blinked, then took a deep drink.

"Do you need me to problem solve this for you?" He fought to suppress a smile. There was no doubt he'd shocked her. But she hadn't refused him. He let his question hang for a few seconds before adding, "Or are you going to do as you're told?"

Avery hesitated for a moment, opening and then closing her mouth.

"I'll go with you," he decided.

"That won't be necessary."

"On the contrary."

He saw the question in her gaze. Then he noticed the way she glanced around the ballroom, seeking out her great-aunt.

When she saw that Miss Scarlet was occupied, Avery nodded.

They left the party to make their way down a long, almost deserted hallway. When she placed a hand on the restroom door, he snagged her wrist to guide her toward a different one, intended for families. He followed her inside, then turned the lock with a decisive *click*. She gasped but didn't protest. Part of him was pissed that she'd come in here with him. "Leaving with a man without telling anyone could be damn dangerous, Layla."

Avery met his gaze with trust he didn't deserve.

Cole longed to rip off her damn mask and have no pretenses between them. "Don't do anything this stupid ever again." Why it bothered him so much, he didn't know. This need to protect her stunned him. "What's your safe word?" His tone had a bite, and that didn't seem to scare her either.

"Red. And I use slow, rather than yellow."

"What's on your limits list?"

"The usual. Permanent markings. Well, I mean, unless there was a long-term relationship in place. Then it might be open to negotiation." She paused. "No breaking my skin. Or humiliation."

"Agreed. There are condoms in my room. If we get that far, it will be completely your choice, and we'll be practicing safe sex."

She nodded. "I'd like that."

His cock was heavy with arousal.

Without him needing to prompt her, she removed her thong. A deep red stained her cheeks when she held out the material toward him.

"Put it in your mouth," he said, rather than accepting it.

She gasped, and the room pulsed with her fear-induced excitement.

With any other woman, he'd go slower. But he was unaccountably annoyed with her pretense. "When I give you an order, sub"—he took a step toward her—"you will obey."

She shivered.

"Unless you need to use a safe word, your acceptable replies are 'yes, Sir,' or 'yes, Cole.'" He dropped his voice. "Master works fine too." That, he wanted to hear.

"I…"

"Do you understand?"

"Yes, Cole."

"From here on, hesitations will be dealt with appropriately. Questions?"

She stuffed her panties into her mouth.

Blood rushed to his dick. She was perfect. He hadn't realized how much he'd missed playing with a sub. "Now I want you spread-eagle, hands on the wall."

Slowly she pivoted and followed his instructions.

"Is your pussy wet?"

Her mumble was hard to hear, but absolutely delightful. "Yes, Sir."

"Do you like it when you're told what to do? When to do it? Do you like being naughty, wondering who saw you walk in here? Are you anxious about what might happen?" He came up behind her, close enough that he inhaled the sharp and unmistakable scent of her arousal. "You should be."

She spread her fingers farther apart.

"I'm going to check to see if you're wet. Am I going to be disappointed?" With the back of his hand, he brushed hair away from her neck. "Or is your slit going to be so damp that I'm pleased?" Her arms trembled. "What will I do if you're not properly responsive? Pinch your thigh?" Through the dress, he did.

She swallowed deep but didn't protest.

"Perhaps I'll lift your dress and spank your bare ass just because I want to."

Avery whimpered, the sound soft and pleading—everything he wanted.

"Perhaps I'll just put one finger in your pussy and another in your ass."

The little sub squirmed.

"I'm not known for my kindness. You should understand that."

In silent challenge, she stuck her ass out a little.

Enchanting, if reckless. "You're much more of a sinner than a saint, aren't you, Layla?" He grabbed a fistful of her gown and yanked it up to her waist. "That's it—push your butt out toward me even more. Give it to me for a spanking."

She didn't hesitate. Instead, she braced herself on the wall, then thrust back, a woman desperate to receive what he was desperate to give.

"Has it been a while?" he asked.

"Yes, Sir." A second later, she confessed, "Too long." The

words were garbled by her makeshift gag, but her response was clear, her plea impossible to deny.

"What do you want?"

"Spank me, Sir."

Rather than delivering what she requested, he worked his hand between her legs to find her hot cunt.

She moaned and let her forehead rest against the elegant wallpaper.

He rubbed three fingers across her shaved pussy, using her dampness to prevent friction. He stroked her clit quicker and quicker, making her legs shake, driving her toward an orgasm before pulling his hand away.

Then because she was so wet, he put one finger against her rear entrance. "Do you like it dirty?" he asked against her ear.

"Yes. Yes, Sir." She groaned.

He loved that she'd shown no hesitation when he'd bared her, toyed with her, pressed a finger to her anus.

When he saw her at the play party, she'd been so much more restrained. Now he realized that was more a result of the man she was with. "Whatever you want," he promised. "Whatever it is. I'll be sure you get it." He eased his finger into her a little.

She inhaled and allowed the wall to support more of her weight. *So fucking hot.*

He pushed past her sphincter and breached her anally. It wasn't as comfortable as if he'd used lube, he knew, but she didn't protest.

Cole worked his finger all the way in, then brought his other hand around to play with her pussy for a couple of seconds. "I'm going to enjoy fucking you later, when your ass is so sore that the sheets hurt your skin."

While holding her still, he spanked her left ass cheek hard.

She went rigid.

"More than you expected?"

"Yes, Sir." Avery turned her head to the side, and he saw that her bright-green eyes were wide, unblinking.

"Less than you can take?"

She squeezed her eyes closed and nodded.

"Less than you hoped for?"

He saw her fingers curl.

"Yes, Sir," she admitted around the lacy fabric.

With his finger still in her ass, Cole spanked her again and again until she tapped her heels on the marble floor.

She was getting hotter, wetter. And that was the time to stop, when she was frustrated, his to command.

Cole fisted her hair and pulled back her head, forcing her to look at him. "Any doubt who's in charge, sub?"

"You." Her voice caught in a sob. "You are, Sir."

"Correct." Cole slowly extracted his finger, then flipped down her dress.

While he washed his hands, he left her there, frowning but not questioning. At this point, he wouldn't have been surprised if she was furious or puzzled. But one thing was certain—she knew he would control the scene, and she also knew she was safe with him. He'd read her responses, left her wanting.

He dried his hands on one of the cotton towels, then wadded it and tossed it in a wicker basket. "Put your thong in the inside pocket of my jacket."

She pushed away from the wall, then faced him. He offered an arm for her to brace herself on while she rebalanced on the strappy fuck-me sandals.

Slowly she pulled the fabric from her mouth. She locked her gaze on his face, never severing eye contact as she pulled back his lapel, then skimmed her fingers across the fabric, searching for the opening in the lining.

A few seconds later, she tucked her underwear inside. She allowed her palm to linger on his chest.

"Bold move for a sub who didn't have permission to touch her Dominant." He captured her wrist, even though he liked what she did.

"Yes, Master Cole."

"And brave, looking me in the eye."

She didn't take the hint to glance away.

"No apology?"

She didn't respond.

"Are you a brat, Layla?" He flattened his hand on hers. "With me, you don't have to be. I told you I will ensure you get what you need. You can tell me. Talk to me." Again, Cole was tempted to rip off that damn mask. "Be real with me. Trust me with your secrets."

"Thank you for the offer. I appreciate it." Her cheeks were captivatingly pink. But she hesitated before going on. "And thank you for the spanking, Sir."

He sighed. *One step at a time.* "More to come." He released his grip, then straightened his cuff as she dropped her hand. "We should get back."

"What?"

"The food here—even banquet food—is five-star. You need energy for the night ahead."

"What? We just…" She drew her eyebrows together. "You want to eat?"

"Absolutely. I understand steak and lobster is on the menu." He offered his arm.

He watched the war, the frustration in her eyes. She wanted to protest, but she'd heard him, and she'd agreed to obey him.

Even though she pursed her lips, she composed herself, then placed her hand on his arm as they left the restroom together.

CHAPTER THREE

It was the longest, most nerve-racking meal of Avery's life.

She'd hit on Master Cole, and he'd humbled her in the family restroom, driving her to the edge, proving his dominance, leaving her panting for an orgasm.

She'd expected him to take her up to his room, not back to the party. Sitting here, her pussy damp, her underwear in his jacket, was unbearable.

"Is your filet all right?" he asked, putting down his fork after watching her pick at it for a while.

"It's wonderful." The problem wasn't with the steak—it was with Cole's insistence on her revealing her true identity.

Servers cleared the plates. Then the hotel's pastry chef and several helpers wheeled in a stunning cupcake assortment.

The display resembled the staging that had been set up. Each cupcake was topped with a mask or feathers crafted from fondant. On the top tier was a cake fashioned to resemble Miss Scarlet in a burlesque costume.

The star of the hour took to the stage for a few minutes to

thank everyone for coming. "Please enjoy the music and dancing. And indulge in some free champagne, courtesy of Mr. Sterling himself." She lifted an imaginary glass toward someone in the back of the room. "Thank you, darling!"

By the time Avery turned her head, the doorway was vacant. If the hotelier had been there at all, he wasn't there now.

The musicians struck up again, and the waitstaff went to work, offering cupcakes.

She wrinkled her nose and sighed wistfully when a chocolate one with mile-high frosting was offered to her.

"She'll take it," Cole told the waiter, accepting the plate and a fork.

"But—"

"If you want it, eat it. Or have a bite."

She sighed, never taking her eyes off the confection. "It's my weakness."

"We all have one."

"The calories in that thing," she protested, looking at him.

He had a wide, indulgent smile. "What about them?"

"I need to lose a few pounds."

"Do you?"

"I don't?"

"Only if you think so. I like spanking your delectable ass."

She gave the dessert another couple of glances before meeting his steel-gray eyes. When she saw his approval of her, she picked up her fork.

The cupcake machine in the hotel was wonderful, but this…

"I gather you like it?"

"To die for." She dabbed her mouth with a napkin. "Or certainly worth extra exercise for. Maybe I did die and go to heaven. Did I die and go to heaven?"

"Not yet. But soon."

The reminder of what he had planned made her stomach plummet. Nerves getting to her, she pushed the plate away.

Once they'd had coffee, he said, "It's too early for us to leave. How about another dance?"

She loved being in his arms, so she nodded. So much a gentleman, he stood, pulled back her chair, then offered his elbow and led her to the parquet floor. She loved being publicly claimed by this Dom.

Like earlier, she placed a hand on his shoulder. This time, however, his touch wasn't polite. He placed his palm against her back and brought her in close.

Her step faltered, and he tightened his grip to compensate and help her recover. She gave him a smile of gratitude. His lead was competent as he gave her slight nudges that provided unmistakable cues to follow. His skill as a Dominant extended to the dance floor.

When the final notes trailed off, he released her and gave a slight bow.

For the next hour, they danced, conversed with people, watched circus performers and a burlesque preview—including a teaser of the new show Miss Scarlet was debuting next month.

Cole was patient and polite but maddeningly hands-off. Because of the way he'd behaved earlier, she anticipated a constant stream of commands, but he acted as if they were on a casual date while tension built deep inside her.

When the first guests trickled out of the doors, he looked at her with purpose. "Ready to make our escape?"

His words shot nerves through her. "Yes."

He stood, and this time, his grip wasn't just tight—it was possessive. She liked it more than she would have imagined.

It took a few minutes for them to make it to the front of the admirers lined up to talk to Miss Scarlet.

"The party will be going on until the wee hours." She cast

a glance between them. "In case you want to rejoin us once you've worn yourselves out." With a grin, she waved her fan in front of her face.

A gentleman less than half Miss Scarlet's age pinched her bottom. She squealed and turned around.

Avery couldn't hide her laugh.

"She seems to be having a good time."

"She's inspiring."

Cole held out a hand to indicate Avery should go ahead of him. "Did I understand that you have a room here?"

"Yes. Even though I live not too far from here, I splurged." An evening at the Royal Sterling was a rare treat. With its spas, pools, workout room, and unbelievable food, it was a mini-vacation.

"Which of our rooms do you prefer?"

"Yours." So she could make her escape when she was ready. "But I'd like to collect my purse, maybe freshen up a bit. If it suits you, I can meet you in about fifteen minutes."

"No. That doesn't suit me at all," he replied. "We'll go together."

Nerves that had been at a manageable level flooded through her.

When they were alone in the elevator car, he faced her. "We know spankings are on your approved activities list."

"Yes, Sir." She shifted her weight to her right foot.

"Flogging?"

"Yes." The word emerged as a sigh.

"Cane?"

Avery twisted her hands together. "That can fucking hurt. Sir."

"It can," he agreed. "And for the right sub, it can be sublime."

At his words, hunger unfurled. There was nothing she liked more than the exquisite dance of pain so rich it caused a flash of unbridled pleasure. In the wrong hands, the cane was miserable. But Cole was right. There had been one time when she'd found it sublime. "Yes, Sir."

"Is that a yes to the cane?"

"It takes trust. But…" She licked her lips. "It's something I like." There was nothing like its unyielding, expansive sear.

"All in good time," he agreed. "I'll suggest it again later."

Avery nearly melted at his feet, and no doubt he was astute enough to know that. She looked away from him, trying to diminish the influence he had over her.

"Trust goes two ways." He paused. *"Layla."*

It's as if he knows. She sucked in a breath. "Master Cole, please…"

"Why so secretive?"

She watched the numbers for the various floors fly past. "Can we have tonight?" *Let me be bold, someone I'm not. Let me be the sub I dream of. Tonight, just tonight, allow me to be brave.*

The elevator glided to a stop.

"Tonight," he agreed. "Don't count on anything more. I don't like masquerades—literal or figurative. I despise subterfuge."

"Fair enough, Sir." Her breath was shaky as she exhaled in gratitude.

With the heat of his gaze on her rear, she walked down the hallway to her room.

Avery pressed her thumbprint to the scanner to open the door. She sighed. If only she'd been less scattered before leaving. The bed was strewn with clothes, lingerie, purses she'd considered taking, even a new pair of shoes she'd purchased on a whim at one of the hotel's numerous ground-floor shops.

"Do you have any toys with you?"

"An egg-type vibrator. It has a remote control." The expensive Swedish thing had cost a small fortune, and it had been worth every penny. It worked well whether she was teasing her clit or using it internally.

"Excellent. Bring it with you."

She dug both pieces from the bottom of her suitcase and tucked the toy into her clutch. "Can you excuse me for a moment?"

He went to stand by the window, and she headed into the bathroom.

With the door closed behind her, she removed her mask. For a moment, she hardly recognized the bold person staring back at her. This Avery had gotten spanked in the restroom of the Royal Sterling Hotel, had Master Cole's finger up her ass, and was prepared to go back to his room with him—all things she might never have ordinarily done.

"Two minutes, sub. Don't make me come in there."

"Yes, Sir!" Quickly she brushed her hair. Then, stalling in an attempt to steady her nerves, she applied a fresh coat of mascara. After painting her lips a vixen-red color, she replaced the mask.

All that done, she rejoined him.

He stood near the minibar, a small glass bottle of mineral water in hand. "You are worth any wait."

She sucked in a breath.

Cole perused her, eyes deep with appreciation. In that moment, she believed what he said. "You're very kind, Sir."

"I've warned you that kind isn't a word associated with me. Remember that."

Trepidation danced down her spine. How well *did* she know him?

"Ready?"

She curled her hand into a fist in a futile effort to stop her hand from shaking, then dropped the mascara and lipstick into her clutch. For a moment she debated adding other toiletries, then decided against it. No doubt she would be back in her own room in a couple of hours. She closed the flap on her purse and gave him a tight nod.

In the hallway, he said, "Please walk in front of me."

Her insides lurched.

Everything this man did spoke to his understanding and mastery of a sub.

He instructed her to precede him onto the elevator, then from it when they arrived at his floor.

With his burning gaze on her, Avery had never been more aware of her femininity.

Once they were sealed inside his suite and she'd placed her belongings on his desk, he offered her a drink of the mineral water.

Since there was no way to hide her trembling hand, she shook her head.

Cole pressed a button on his docking station. Within a few seconds, smooth instrumental jazz wove a sensual atmosphere.

Avery looked around. Though they had the same luxurious linens on their beds, he had a couple of additional pieces of furniture, higher ceilings, a wet bar, and an additional window. "You have a lot more space than I do." She just hoped that when she returned to her room there would be chocolate-covered strawberries on her nightstand as well.

"I have a house about thirty minutes from here, but when Sterling offered me a room for the duration of the project, I decided to skip the daily commute." He shrugged. "The fitness center is world class."

"I sometimes think I shouldn't stay here. Going home afterward is always a letdown. Don't get me wrong, my apartment is nice. But it's small. It's not on the Strip. And it doesn't have a cupcake machine." If that wasn't enough to convince her, the twenty-four-hour room service and someone to do her laundry certainly was.

"That should be remedied."

"I've suggested it to management numerous times."

He grinned. "We should enjoy as many of Sterling's amenities as we can. The armoire is unlocked. Have a look inside." His statement was flat, with no inflection. It wasn't a suggestion.

Her legs felt wobbly in a way that had nothing to do with her heels.

She crossed the room to open the doors of the piece of furniture, then stared in wide-eyed shock. He had every impact device imaginable, from floggers to paddles, carpet beaters to crops and canes. Even a single-tail hung curled from a hook.

"This is some collection."

"The Royal Sterling caters to every need."

"So… These aren't yours?"

"Some are. The cane for example." He joined her. "And the short red flogger."

She wanted it on her skin.

"You asked for tonight," he reminded her. "In return, I will demand your total honesty in every other way."

She faced him. "I'm not sure I understand."

"When I ask a question, I want an answer. I've told you that you'll get what you want from me, but you need to be clear about what it is. I expect you to be completely honest."

Avery squared her shoulders, drawing from the strength that anonymity gave her.

"Good." He took a seat in an easy chair, then propped an ankle on the opposite knee. "Please remove your dress."

Taking off her clothes in front of a man for the first time always made her heart careen.

He pressed his hands together and looked at her. There was only a tiny zipper near the base of her spine, and she grabbed the pull tab to slowly lower it.

She brushed the one strap from her shoulder, then allowed the bodice to drop.

She was braless, and his gaze lingered on her breasts. Because of the cool air, her nipples hardened instantly. Or at least that was what she told herself, rather than believing it happened because of the way he watched her.

Without further encouragement, she pulled off her dress. She draped the material across the foot of the bed. "What about the shoes?"

"I like them. But it's up to you. If they're comfortable enough, leave them on. If you feel more like my little sub when you're naked and barefoot, take them off."

"I'll keep them on." Uncertain, she waited for his next instruction.

"Do whatever feels natural."

She clutched her necklace for inner strength. Thoughts tumbled through her, and she took a breath. Deep down, she knew what he expected. A moment later, she knelt.

"Yes," he whispered.

She spread her knees wide and placed her hands behind her neck before tipping back her head and closing her eyes.

"Very nice."

He allowed time to drag and stretch. She forced herself not to fidget. A full minute or so later, she realized—*fuck it*—that he was waiting on her. "Please, Sir, will you touch me?"

"I'm sorry?"

"Will you please touch your sub?" she amended.

"I'd be happy to. In what way?"

If she were Avery Fisher rather than a brave incognito woman, she would never be able to continue this way—asking, taking. But tonight, she could be the sub she dreamed of being. "Will you inspect your sub, Sir?"

"Very well done."

She opened her eyes to see him walking toward her.

Within seconds, he stood over her, deliciously imposing. Slowly, he circled her.

"I like you on your knees, sub."

"Thank you, Sir."

He yanked her hair back, exposing her neck, making her open her mouth. God, this was everything she imagined.

He put his finger on her lips.

"Please may I suck it, Sir?" It stunned her to realize just how much she actually wanted to.

"You may."

As if it were his cock, she circled his finger with her tongue, then drew his finger into her mouth, sucking, licking, adoring.

"Show me your breasts."

Since he hadn't pulled away, she continued to suck while she pushed them together.

He extracted his finger. "What are you thinking?"

"That I'd like you to fuck them, Sir—my breasts—maybe come on them."

"You are a sexy woman, Layla." He placed his hands on hers, forcing her breasts even closer together.

She moaned a little.

"What else needs inspection?"

"My cunt, Sir." Then instantly, she corrected, "Your sub's cunt, Sir."

"You were reminded once, earlier. Weren't you?"

Her pulse stuttered. "Yes, Sir."

"I think the lapse should be punished."

"Please, Sir." *Please, please, yes.*

"Slap your cunt."

"Sir?"

"You seem to think it belongs to you. Therefore you should be the one to punish it."

Stunned by the order, she looked at him. He wasn't going to do it for her?

"Are you waiting for something?" He took a step back to give her some space.

Despite the chill in the room, her body was hot. Having no other choice, she slapped her pussy. The pain surprised her.

"You might have better access if your legs were spread farther apart." His words sounded like a suggestion, and she knew they were anything but.

"Yes, Sir." She followed his order and gave herself a second slap, then a third. "How many, Sir?"

He shrugged. "How many would you like?"

They were playing a sinful game she could never win. "As many as you say, Sir."

"Ah." He smiled.

This man tested everything she knew about BDSM.

Because he hadn't said she could stop, she kept going—two more, three, four… *It damn well stings.*

Her pussy became inflamed. And because she was submissive and there was nothing hotter than having a powerful Dom looming over her, commanding her actions, she started to get wet.

She lost track. All she knew was that her pussy was unbelievably sensitive.

"If it were my pussy, it would get a different kind of attention."

She frowned at him. "Sir?"

He continued to regard her, and she continued to spank until fresh realization dawned. "Show me," she invited. "Show your sub how you would treat your pussy, Sir."

"Fuck."

For a moment, she thought he might use her real name, but that wasn't possible.

"Please stand and put your hands behind you."

Her motions weren't as graceful as they might have been if she'd recently had a Dom and routinely knelt. But he didn't complain. In fact, he smiled as though he approved of her actions.

He took a step in her direction, and she sucked in a breath. She was hyperaware of him. His stance communicated power and command.

"Wet my fingers." He held his hand in front of her face, and she licked them as she continued to meet his gaze.

He slid his hand between her legs and teased her, slipping his fingers in and out of her pussy, driving her mad.

She closed her eyes. The soft pumping of his fingers coupled with the sharp smacks she'd given herself made her delirious.

Tremors shook her as she imagined what she looked like, naked except for her gorgeous mask, the necklace, and high-heeled sandals, breasts thrust out, shoulder blades drawn together, hands behind her neck, legs spread. Surrendered to his mercy.

He removed his hand and she moaned.

But then he slapped her cunt so hard that she screamed, lost her balance, and pitched forward.

He caught her. "Back into position."

She couldn't. "The pain..." She squeezed her thighs together, desperate to escape the burning sensation. "Damn. Damn. *Fuck.*"

"*That's* how I would treat my pussy."

Avery gulped, but shockingly once the searing pain receded, pleasure flooded her. She'd never been more sexually aroused than she was at that moment. God. It wasn't enough. Avery thrust her hips forward, seeking his hand and the release an orgasm would bring.

"Back into position," he repeated.

She realized she was gripping his forearms and that he'd leaned in to offer his body as support. Without her being aware of it, he'd been there for her. "Thank you," she whispered.

Slowly, she righted herself. Momentarily she closed her eyes to reenter the submissive mindset.

"Now show me...show me how you should spank it next time I ask."

He expects me to do that to myself? There was no way she could bear it. For a wild second, she considered using her safe word. But then... She knew she might never have another night like this one or a second chance to play with Master Cole.

"I'm waiting."

"Yes, Sir." Harder than she could have imagined, she did as he said.

On top of the pain she'd already experienced, this was stunning. Before she could sort through the emotional ramifications, he was there, an arm around her waist, stroking her labia, easing a finger inside her.

She gulped for air, feeling as if she were drowning. "Sir!"

"Come anytime you want," he said against her ear, the words gruff and simultaneously promising.

He slipped a second finger inside her. The sensation was hot, fucking hot. Then he inserted a third and spread them apart, fucking her hard and deep. Her pussy blazed in response to his sensual assault.

She wrapped her arms around his neck so she could stay upright. Seconds later, a climax shot through her, its intensity shocking.

Avery's body went limp, and he picked her up. Without her being fully conscious of what was happening, he carried her to the chair where he sat and drew her against him.

She curled up, accepting his comfort, heedless that she was naked.

This Dom understood her, what she needed, maybe even on a level she didn't quite comprehend herself. "That was…" She sought for the right description, but words failed her. "Sexy."

"You like it hard."

"Yes." Something inside her blossomed. Allowing herself to be honest was liberating.

"When you're ready, I want you on your knees."

She remained where she was for another minute or two, soothed by the sound of his pounding heart, the strength of his arms, the masculine scent of him.

Being with him was so natural, easy in a way she'd never experienced with anyone else. Eventually she was able to rouse herself enough to slide from his lap to kneel on the floor.

"Undress me. Except for my pants."

Anticipation flooded her. Not that things hadn't been real before now, but this command magnified his power.

Avery started with his shoes, untying the laces of each of expensive wingtip. This part of BDSM helped her center herself. She enjoyed simple tasks that she could treat reverently. In a way, it was meditative.

Once she'd removed his shoes and tucked the socks inside, he stood, again towering over her, making her deliciously aware of her submissive pose.

His eyes were lighter than they'd been earlier, molten. Intimacy whispered around them.

"I'm waiting." He offered his hand and helped her up.

She moved behind him to take his jacket. As he shrugged from it, she noticed that her thong peeked out from one of his pockets, and she absently wondered if he had any intention of returning it.

Not that it mattered. Part of her hoped he'd want to keep it.

"There's a wooden hanger in the closet."

She hung the jacket, then smoothed imaginary wrinkles from it. That done, she returned to unfasten his bowtie.

The image of him with the ends loose against the snowy-white shirt would remain with her for years.

Avery removed his studs, then his cufflinks, noting the owl on each of them. Finally, she unfastened the remaining two buttons on his tuxedo shirt.

Again she went behind him to help him from the shirt.

His back, with honed muscles and a couple of badly healed scars, took her breath away. She had labeled him a secret-agent man, and of course there was his military background. How much didn't she know? Judging by the fact that he was consulting for the Royal Sterling, there was no doubt Cole didn't sit at a desk all day.

She hung the shirt next to his jacket in the closet and tucked his tie into the same pocket as her underwear; then she looked at him, drinking in the sight of his lean stomach and slender waist. His chest had a smattering of hair, and she couldn't stop staring at his biceps.

Even though a smile toyed with his mouth, his tone was stern. "Hurry up, sub. Unless you want to be chastised for tarrying?"

Damn, she loved being with a Dominant who made it easy for her to be the sub she wanted to be.

"What does intuition tell you to do now?" he asked.

With any other Dom, she might respond as expected, with the perfect, *"Whatever you say, Sir."* But tonight was different. Tonight she was asking for what she wanted. "If it pleases you, Sir…I'd like to suck your dick."

He inclined his head a little. "There are condoms in the

nightstand." With his thumb, he indicated the piece of furniture. "Crawl to it and bring one to me."

Avery found quite a selection, all of the shiny packages emblazoned with the Sterling's crown logo. She dug through the small bowl they were in until she located one without spermicide.

She started to crawl to him, but his words stopped her.

"Put it in your mouth."

It was uncomfortable, and she wanted to spit it out, but she didn't dare. Her eyes watered as she made her way toward him, and she fought her gag reflex while she unfastened his belt.

"Think about what you're doing and not about your discomfort," he encouraged. "Get out of your own head."

She tugged on the thin, supple strip of leather, pulling it from around his waist.

After coiling it, she set it aside.

Then she unfastened the single button and lowered the zipper on his pants.

For a moment, she held her breath, wondering if he was commando. But he wasn't. Cole wore tight dark boxer briefs. His cock jutted against them. Even though he was confined, there was no doubt he was well-endowed. Maybe *too* well-endowed. What had she been thinking when she'd offered to suck him off?

She lowered his pants, and once he'd stepped free of them, she picked them up and folded them, then offered them to him.

"You've either had some good training or you have remarkably good instincts."

She nodded.

"Which is it? The training?"

The condom package made her choke, preventing speech.

"Mostly instinct, then, hmm? I prefer that. I like to train my women to my preferences."

The idea of being his woman, his sub, made her heart race. What would that be like? Not to simply have a scene on the weekends, but to live the lifestyle more often, even daily? To have her days filled with little acts of service to her man? To have him demand dirty things from her, to compel her obedience? Avery forced away the exhilarating questions. They had tonight and no more.

He took the pants from her, then hung them on the back of the chair, undoing her careful work.

She hooked her fingers inside the waistband of his underwear and pulled down the material. His cock sprang free, jutting toward her face. He was magnificent and definitely on the large side. But the fact that he was already hard sent a flash of pleasure through her.

She finished undressing him, appreciating the way he'd trimmed his pubic hair and shaved his balls. Everything about him signaled his awareness of his sexuality. If the condom package hadn't been stuck in her mouth, she would have been tempted to start sucking now.

"I love the sight of a woman who's helpless to me. Put the condom on me."

Nerves crawled through her, forcing her to concentrate hard on what she was doing. Being this close to him—drinking in his masculinity—overwhelmed her. She couldn't resist touching his testicles and sucking his cock deep into her throat.

Cole fisted her hair. "Do as you're told."

She wanted *this*. He tightened his grip, forcing her compliance. "Yes, Sir." Avery ripped open the package and sheathed him.

"You did that well."

"Thank you, Sir."

"But you took liberties without asking permission."

Her pulse lurched.

"You know better, I presume?"

"Uhm." The temperature of the room dropped by ten chilling degrees. "I…"

"Do you?" He raised an eyebrow.

"Sir…"

"Do you?" His voice whiplashed through her.

"Yes, Sir!" She glanced away. "I do."

"And you're supposed to be asking tonight, talking to me about your desires."

Also true.

"Fetch the flogger."

Oh God. Prior to him, she had never been punished in a BDSM scene.

But then, she'd never been with a man as uncompromising and stern as Master Cole. Fuck. *Yes.* This. This was what she'd always wanted. But that didn't stop sudden terror from seizing her.

"Do I need to repeat my order?"

If it became too much, she had a safe word. Her movements were sluggish as she crawled to the armoire. She stood, then opened the doors and selected the flogger. Again, on her knees, she returned to him, sat back on her heels, then offered the implement to him.

He was so imposing with his throbbing erection that it was difficult to think.

"Anything you want to say?"

This was so real, so raw. "I'm sorry, Sir." She peeked through the curtain of her unfamiliar blonde hair. "No—" Avery cleared her throat so she could speak. "That's not true. You want honesty? I should have asked, waited for your command. But I'm not sorry I touched you."

"Thank you for being truthful." His voice was rich, like a fine red wine, and just as potent. "That will help you some."

Some?

"Go back to the armoire and stand in front of it, facing it. Put your hands on the top and spread your legs as wide as you can." He paused. "I recommend you be quick about it."

CHAPTER FOUR

Captivated, Cole watched Avery follow his order. Her motions were graceful, innately so. Her touch and her mouth were exquisite. Part of him ached to make love to her. But that wasn't what she wanted.

Typically, he didn't flog women when he had a raging hard-on. Then again, he'd never had an evening like this.

He allowed her tension to build for a couple of minutes before going to her. The moment he was close, she drew in a short, frantic breath. He trailed his fingers across her shoulders, down her spine, over her shapely buttocks. "You've got the most spankable ass of any woman I've ever known."

"It's the cupcakes, Sir."

"Then I shall hire us a pastry chef."

She glanced over her shoulder.

"You're divine," he said. "And don't think that means I won't make you too sore to sit down."

She moaned a little as she faced forward again.

He scooped her hair to one side. "I want you to consider yourself tied."

"My Doms usually cuff me, Sir."

"At what point did you confuse me with anyone else?" He grabbed her ass cheeks and squeezed hard, lifting her off her heels.

She gasped, more from shock than pain, he supposed, since his touch hadn't been heavy-handed.

"Oh, God! I'm sorry, Sir."

"Better." He slowly released his grip, and her exhalation was so ragged even her shoulders shook.

It was good to know he affected her in the same way she was getting to him.

He rubbed her body with long, slow, forceful strokes, getting her blood flowing, letting her know he was in charge. "You asked for this." With her words, her body, her actions, she'd been clear about it. "Stay in place. Make me proud of you."

"That's a difficult task, Sir."

"I think you want me to demand a lot from you." She didn't immediately respond. "That's why you approached me. Be truthful." *About this, if nothing else.*

"Yes," she whispered, her words husky with confession.

Fuck. It was a start. Yet it made him want more. "You can count, if you want. I'll stop when I'm ready or when you use a safe word."

Her muscles tensed. Was it from anticipation or the slight fear he was trying to cultivate? "Surrender to me. To yourself." He touched her, soothed her until she exhaled. "Good." He gave her a few gentle strikes on her perfect buttocks. He was not concerned that he might lose his erection. The sight of her skin turning color beneath the supple strands of his flogger would be enough to keep him aroused.

Cole continued to work her with light strokes until her muscles relaxed, draining the tension from her.

Only then did he start the flogging in earnest.

As they connected, breathed in sync, he realized how

much he'd missed this. The last year he'd spent with Gia had consisted of half a dozen emotional meltdowns. She'd believed that once they moved in together, he would be home more, even though he'd said he wouldn't be. She resorted to bratty behavior to get his attention. Twice, he returned from overseas trips to discover she'd moved back in with her parents. She wanted him to chase her. Far too often, he did. She treated him and their relationship as some sort of game.

He'd worked with her, asking her to talk with him. Instead, she'd left him guessing. Toward the end, he stopped responding to her dramatics. The next time she stormed out, he didn't pursue her. Three days later, angry, accusing him of not loving her enough, she returned. For a while, things had gotten better, but then she started avoiding sex.

He'd been wrong to think he could stop her manipulations.

The fourth time she moved out, he changed the locks.

Cole finished his case, then volunteered for extra assignments. He'd avoided relationships since.

While he was abstinent, he'd spent a lot of time in reflection and decided he only wanted to be with women who were self-aware and willing to ask for what they needed. The time he'd already spent with Avery meant a great deal to him, made him think about the future and maybe the sound of laughter in his ridiculously big house.

Appearing relaxed, she rested her head on the armoire. For a moment he stopped, and she shifted her weight from foot to foot. He traced a faint mark on her creamy skin. "How are you doing?"

She attempted to lift her head, only to drop it again. "Wonderful."

He trailed his touch lower to check her arousal level.

"If this is supposed to teach me to ask before touching you, Sir, I'm not sure it's working."

Cole grinned. "If it had been a real punishment, you'd know the difference."

"I'm sure you're right, Sir."

He fucking loved the sound of his title on her tongue. There were a dozen different inflections he wanted to hear. Pleading. Surrendering. Screaming. "Would you like to continue?"

"Please."

Cole crisscrossed her body, using complete strokes, wrapping the strands around her, from her thighs to her buttocks to her waist.

Following his commands, Avery didn't release the piece of furniture, but she readjusted her grip for more support. Despite that, her breaths were rhythmic and deep. Her skin was a tantalizing pink, and her knees wobbled a little. "Talk to me."

"I want to get lost."

"Be specific, please."

"I want it harder."

It wouldn't have mattered to him if she wanted to stop. But her request for more pleased him. His cock was still hard, reminding him how long he'd been without sex.

Cole gave her another twenty strokes. When she sighed with pleasure, he unleashed a little more strength to finish her with a deeper impact.

She swayed, her body relaxed.

Avery had been worth every minute of the wait.

He paused for a moment, flogger at his side, while he fingered her.

Cole threaded both hands into her hair to turn her head to one side. Wanting her, he kissed her, cradling her head in his palm. He was tender, more than he'd ever been with a sub. Her submission cracked the ice around his heart—as a man, not just a Dom.

She tasted of honesty, of the finest champagne, of compliance. Her mouth was soft, her tongue yielding.

And because he was feasting on her response, Cole pulled away from her. He shook his head to clear it. A kiss was incredibly intimate. And with her, one would not be enough. So what the hell was he doing? They'd agreed to a single night and nothing more. Tied in knots, annoyed with himself, he said, "Now…now you can suck my cock."

Cole helped her turn; then he put his hand on top of her head to force her down onto her knees.

She appeared to be in a stupor, from endorphins, from confusion, and he savored it. "Since you used your hands earlier without permission, put them behind your neck and open your mouth." He stroked himself a couple of times while she did as she was told. "Now satisfy me."

She swirled her tongue across his cockhead, then began to lick, pressing her tongue against the underside.

He curled a fist around his dick to control how much she took. "Open wider, sub." Beneath her mask, he saw her green eyes water as he went deeper. If her mascara ran, so much the better. He held the back of her head to prevent her from escaping.

Properly responsive, she choked on him but didn't pull away, taking everything he offered and continuing to move her tongue and suck.

"Enough." He captured her chin with his hand.

When he pulled away, she didn't even try to wipe her mouth. Instead, she looked up with eyelashes fringed with tears. Damn, he wanted more than the measly hours she was offering. "Sexy. Fucking sexy." He helped her to stand. Then before she could walk past him, he put a hand on her shoulder to stop her.

"Sir?"

Cole grabbed his shirt, and he used the bottom of it to clean her mouth.

"I actually liked it, Sir," she said.

His cock pulsed in demand, and she stared at it. Harsher than he needed to be, he clipped out, "On the bed."

She sat on the edge of the mattress while he collected the bowtie from his suit coat.

"Give me your wrists," he instructed. "This will help you to remember to pay attention to your hands." He secured her with his bowtie. The material was slick, and it would open with the slightest effort, but his intent wasn't to prevent movement. It was to make her conscious of his will. He tipped her back as he said, "Spread your legs."

Though she was already aroused, Cole played with her pussy, fingering her again, even as he pumped his still-sheathed cock in his left hand. "Are you ready for me?"

"I am. Yes, Sir."

He said nothing.

She lifted her head off the mattress as best she could, seeking his gaze. "I'm asking. Please put your dick in me, Sir."

Grateful there had already been turndown service, he moved her to the middle of the mattress with her arms over her head.

He took a minute to lave her nipples with attention, tormenting them, causing her to lift her hips from the bed.

"I'm so ready to come, Sir."

"Are you?" He hoped he sounded nonchalant, because in truth he was anything but.

With his knee, he forced her legs farther apart. Then because her pussy was so red and swollen, he slapped it hard.

She screamed, and he leaned over her, placing his cock at her opening and capturing her cry with his mouth.

He devoured her, and she thrashed about. Sexily, her pussy drenched his dick as he slid in.

Cole tried to soften the kiss, but she met his tongue thrust for thrilling thrust. He'd encouraged her to ask for what she wanted. She responded with a demand.

He pulled back, and she moaned. As he fucked her with short, fast strokes designed to drive her mad, her sound became a whimper.

She moved with him and closed her eyes.

His sub struggled against the makeshift bondage and turned her head to the side, breaking their kiss.

"Master Cole, I want to come."

"You don't need permission." He reached between them to press her engorged clit. "*Now.*"

She cried out his name as she climaxed, clenching his cock with her internal muscles.

Cole ground his back teeth together to fight off his orgasm. He'd never been with a woman as exquisite as Avery, and the struggle was more than he'd anticipated. He had to dig deep into his military training to find a thought that would distract him.

He pulled out from her a little, needing time to regroup.

When she stared up at him, he stroked into her again.

"I didn't know it could be so good."

Big, strong, tough, hardened Dom that he was, he had no fucking idea how to admit that he hadn't known either. "The night is ours."

Her eyes were wide.

"Stop hiding from me?" He touched the top of her mask and traced one of the delicate lines.

She turned her head to escape.

Cole sighed. Even though it went against his better instincts, he'd promised anonymity.

This time as he fucked her, he set a more leisurely pace so he could prolong her pleasure.

"I need to touch you," she said.

"You can get out of that tie anytime."

"We both know that I wouldn't do that, Sir."

"What a good little sub."

Her green eyes were like sun-drenched gems. And her delicate mouth was parted. She wanted to be obedient. He'd been wrong in his casual assumption that she might be a brat. She was simply a woman who yearned for a man strong enough to accept her gifts.

He clamped a hand on her delicate wrists.

"I learned my lesson earlier, Sir. They'll stay where they are until you say otherwise."

He could fuck her all night long. But it wouldn't be enough.

With long, penetrating strokes, he slid in and out of her, ignoring the demanding fullness in his balls. "Look at me." There was something incredibly powerful about compelling a submissive to meet his gaze. But when his little sub did, he wondered who was truly enslaved by whom. He wanted her as much as she obviously wanted him.

He fucked her tight channel, and she sighed.

For minutes, he continued to watch her reactions. As she became more aroused, she blinked less often, and she opened her mouth a little. Her lipstick had already been worn off by their passion. Her compliance was so damn beautiful.

Primal urges obliterated his restraint, and he began to fuck her in earnest.

Whatever he gave, she responded, hard and fast, short and sweet, leisurely and prolonged.

It unraveled his self-control.

He moved them both so she was half on her side, a leg on top of his, giving him leverage to penetrate deeper.

Then, because he wanted to, he plucked the knot from the bowtie.

"May I?"

"Yes. Touch me."

Instantly she grabbed him, holding his shoulders, wrapping herself around him.

Though he liked having his lover restrained to remind them both of the overarching nature of their relationship, he liked the feel of her hands exploring him.

She curved her body, inviting him in deeper. Obligingly, he filled her heated pussy.

"I love this," she said. "Fuck me hard, Sir."

He gave her what she asked for, one hand tangled in her hair, the other pressed flat against her buttocks to prevent her from moving far.

Her pussy muscles squeezed him tight. He fisted his hands to hold off longer, wanting her to climax first.

"Sir!"

"Come."

She screamed, clenching, coming, grabbing him.

He savored each second that he satisfied his sub.

Only when she was whimpering his name did he allow himself to ejaculate in long, satisfying spurts.

He was a sexual man, masturbating at least once a day, and most times, more. But there was no feeling that matched coming inside a responsive woman.

Inside her.

When he was finished, he framed her face between his palms. "You're stunning..." He barely stopped himself from using her name.

"That was hot, Sir. Can we do it again?"

"You'll be the death of me." Suddenly he wasn't afraid of dying.

Avery had never been much of a snuggler, but she didn't object when he returned to the bed after throwing away the condom and pulled her against his naked body. He didn't ask—he just wrapped her up in the strength and comfort of his arms. She lay next to him, listening to the reassuring beat of his heart.

She smiled, glad she'd found the guts to approach him earlier in the evening. Their time together had been everything she could have imagined.

The only problem was much the same as the one she had with staying at the Royal Sterling. It was difficult to go back to the regular world.

Unlike other Doms she'd scened with, Cole seemed to understand the emotional component she needed. To her, it was about more than just kinky sex or having her ass warmed at the club or occasional parties. She wanted the mindfuck and escape. She wanted someone who understood her—or, better, the sub she yearned to be. The person Dirk had told her was wrong.

Cole trailed his fingers down her arm. "How does your body feel?"

He was big, and his thrusts were powerful. "My pussy aches," she admitted with a blush.

A chuckle rumbled through his chest. "Good. And the rest of your body from the flogging?"

"Warm." He'd wielded the leather strands with confidence and the power she needed. "Relaxed."

"Oh?"

"Fishing for compliments?" She turned to face him with a teasing grin. "You know you're good."

His face was shadowed with midnight-dark stubble that appealed to her. Though his jaw was strong, his smile was transformative. Unable to resist—helpless to keep her hands to herself—she traced the scar on his face. Surprisingly, he didn't stop her.

The raised white line ran deeper than she'd imagined. It was an outward manifestation of the risk he'd taken in his life, so different from her sheltered upbringing.

How many layers are there to this Dom?

"Just making sure I take care of my woman."

The words poured heat through her. *His woman.* She liked that, wished it were true. "I enjoyed it more than any other flogging I've received. You're a master."

"Go on."

She sighed, thinking through what she wanted to say. "The way you started told me I could trust you. By the time you hit me harder and faster, I was ready. I think on some level I was aware that it hurt, but I didn't really feel it." Even to her, that statement made no sense, but he nodded in apparent understanding. "You could have continued a lot longer, and it would have been fine with me."

"You've still got a caning to go."

She froze. "Master Cole."

"If you want it," he added.

"I…" Avery recalled the way he'd been with Gia—tenderness, combined with the indomitable force of his Dominance.

"Bring it to me when you're ready."

"I'm nervous," she admitted.

"And?" He arched his eyebrows.

She blew out a breath. "You seem supremely unconcerned."

"I am. I'm looking forward to seeing marks on your thighs and buttocks. If you're fortunate, you'll feel them for some time."

Leaving the comfort of his arms was one of the more

difficult things she'd ever done. But the temptation was irresistible.

Without being instructed, she crawled to the armoire to collect the cane.

"Your vibrator also." He climbed from the bed.

She rummaged through her purse until she found the small egg and its remote control, then returned to him.

Cole pulled his trousers on, and there was something illicit about her Dom being dressed while she was nude.

From her knees a few feet in front of him, she turned her palms up and offered both toys to him.

"I want you bent over the bed. Do you need to be restrained?"

That offer was a small mercy, and she appreciated it. She was honest when she said, "Whatever you prefer, Sir."

"In that case, no. I want your ass in the correct position because you want this as badly as I do."

Her mouth dried.

"Spread your legs as far apart as possible."

Fighting her nerves, she went to the bed, then draped herself across the mattress and turned her head to watch him.

He put the bullet in his mouth to lubricate it, then pressed it against her swollen pussy. She moaned and swayed, allowing it to slip inside her.

Using the remote control, he turned it on to a slow, frustrating pulse. She generally went straight to the highest setting.

"How's that?"

She wrinkled her nose. "Irritating more than anything."

"Distracting?"

"Yes, Sir."

"Good. I'll give you more when I'm ready."

It pulsed again, and she felt it in her belly. "Now's a good time."

Her evil Dom laughed. "I'm sure it is. Close your legs please."

When the vibe pulsed again, she moved her hips, trying to stimulate her clitoris. Having her thighs together increased the sensations and prevented her from getting any friction. "This is borderline mean."

"Nothing borderline about it, sub." He rubbed her skin.

She squeezed her muscles, dreading the horrid stripes that would follow.

Undaunted, he covered her ass cheeks and thighs with a dozen blazing slaps.

By the time he caught her with the first light smack from the cane, she was ready to climb out of her mind.

He gave her numerous taps that she figured were designed to increase her resistance and pain threshold. She wasn't stupid enough to think he was going to continue to be so gentle.

Suddenly the vibration inside her increased. She murmured in protest.

"Ready?"

Before she responded, he cut into her upper thigh with a brutal strike that only the cane could deliver.

She hissed.

"I take it you felt that one?" He turned the dial.

A long pulse went through her only to gently fade to nothing. "I hate that setting."

"Because?"

Avery struggled for words. Was it possible for him to understand something she'd never tried to articulate? "It feels as if I'm being wound up. When I reach the pinnacle, ready for more, it's gone."

"Ah."

He made no move to change it, even though she expected that he would. "Sir?"

"I told you to ask."

She nodded.

"I never promised to give in to you. I said you will receive everything you need."

"That's fucked-up." *And not for the first time.*

"Dominance and submission." He marked her again.

Avery buried her head into the mattress to ensure she didn't scream.

"Take it." Cole laid another nasty stripe above the first.

She exhaled.

The third felt vicious. Combined with the whirling inside her pussy, she couldn't relax.

"Settle in."

Easy for him to say when it wasn't his ass in the air waiting for the evil rattan to be delivered.

An intimidating whistle sliced the air before the implement connected with her right buttock. She pitched forward, and he increased the torment inside her, making her forget the pain.

He moved on to her left cheek, searing it.

In her experience, there was nothing like the cane. It humbled. Its radiating bite went deep, and it didn't dissipate as fast as a flogger's.

But the vibrator changed her relationship with the pain, helping her to disassociate.

"Three more," he stated.

She'd be lucky to take two.

"Unclench your fingers, sub. Just relax."

Avery hadn't realized she was desperately wadding the sheet in her fists. It took all of her concentration to release her grasp.

"Don't fight. Breathe. It is what it is. In and out."

She nodded.

This time, he placed one beneath her butt cheeks in that tender, perfect strike zone.

"Damn."

He massaged the skin he'd tormented, and her muscles softened, allowing her to accept more.

"Where would you like the next?"

"I wouldn't."

"Slow? Red?"

She exhaled. "No." She'd be proud of herself for getting through this. "On my ass cheeks, Sir?"

"That's what I was hoping you'd say."

He laid one on her, and she gulped back a cry.

Her legs wobbled. She was grateful to be over the bed. If he'd asked her to hold the armoire, she would have fallen over.

He gave her some time to process the pain, file it away.

Then he turned up the vibrator.

He continued to interact with her, touching, massaging, kissing, and she began to slip away. She was aware of him talking to her, but at some point, pleasure vanquished every other feeling. The high from the endorphins wrapped around her. Each stripe from the cane only gave her a new feeling of bliss.

Then she was aware of nothing, just a soothing, enveloping sensation, much like being in a warm bath.

"Well done."

She heard the words but didn't comprehend them, didn't respond to them.

Cole moved back her hair and kissed the side of her neck. "You are an exquisite play partner."

When she opened her eyes, she was sitting up in bed, the comforter wrapped around her bare shoulders, nestled in the crook of Cole's arm. He'd even managed to extract the bullet.

"You're back?"

"Yeah." Her own whisper was too loud. For some reason, all her senses seemed heightened.

"How are you feeling?"

"Incredible." It had to have been her state of otherworldliness that drove her confession. Everything she'd fantasized about had come true. She'd slipped free from the constraints of her body and moved someplace inviting. *Subspace.* Words didn't exist to explain it—the thrill, the way reality fragmented, and the brightness of colors, sensation of soaring through time and space.

The journey had been more exhilarating than she'd dared hope. His exquisite care and tender, infinite patience completed the experience.

He reached toward the nightstand to pick up the bottle of mineral water. "You'll need this."

She accepted it, and he kept his hand cupped beneath it, just in case her grip was still unsteady.

After swallowing a couple of sips, she gave the drink back. Her hand *was* shaking.

"Did you enjoy being someone different for the evening?"

Avery put her hand flat on his chest and pushed herself away from him as much as possible. "Sir?" She frowned.

"Someone you're not usually. Bolder? Braver?"

Her pulse sped, then slowed. "Yes."

His gaze was steely, uncompromising. "How difficult was it?"

"I'm not sure I understand the question, Sir."

"Admitting what you wanted. Asking for it. Did you like it?"

She scowled, confused, his clipped tone making her wary. "Yes."

"Then it's time for you to be completely honest. Take off the mask."

"Don't." Avery reached up to hold it in place. "That's not part of our agreement."

"We fit together well. I'd like to see you again, but in order for that to happen, there can be no secrets between us."

Her world became quicksand.

"I had a sub who resorted to manipulation to get her needs met. Games. Brattiness. Anything to catch my attention and keep it focused on her."

Pain cut through his words, but Avery had her own demons. "I didn't ask for more than one night," she reminded him, even while she fantasized about a thousand more.

"You're a beautiful sub...*Layla.*"

There it was again, that pause.

"And you can have what you want. It takes daring, a big risk. But what are the alternatives? A lifetime of hiding who you really are? Being frustrated? There are costs to your choices."

"There are costs to everything. Asking for too much. *Being* too much." Holding a sheet to her breasts, she bolted from the mattress and snatched up her gown.

He climbed from the bed, spectacular and overwhelming. "The next time I see you, it will be without pretense. No mask. No hiding. Every secret laid bare before me."

What the hell have I gotten myself into? "There won't be a next time." She struggled to get into her dress.

"Let me."

"You've done enough."

"I said *let me.*" His eyes were chilly, like a winter's day.

Damn him and his domineering ways.

Without waiting for another argument, he took the dress from her and raised it over her head.

Once it was in place, she exhaled and reached back to fasten it.

He brushed aside her shaky hands and raised the zipper.

"Thank you." This wasn't ending the way she'd envisioned, with her mysteriously slipping from his bed in the middle of the night. She hated the way they were parting.

Cole picked up her vibrator and remote and offered them to her. "You can reach me through Diana or Alcott. Or call the hotel and ask to be put through." He shrugged. "And you know which room I'm staying in, if you wish to present your ass for a spanking."

That won't be happening. "Thanks for the fuck, Mr. Stewart."

He grabbed her by the shoulders, his jaw tight. His fingers bit into her skin. "It was more than a fuck for me. And it was to you as well, and that's why you're running scared. I'll tell you this—you'll remember tonight. You'll think about it. You may be with someone else, but you'll want this. And you won't be able to have it unless, and until, you stop running."

Pain seared her lungs, but she refused to let him see her distress.

She pulled away, crossed the room to grab her clutch, then stuffed her sex toy inside. Without a look back, she left, pulling the door closed with a decisive click.

Only then did she collapse against the wall.

She put a hand to her throat and drew a couple of breaths to tamp down the adrenaline. How the hell had the evening gone from something so perfect to a stunning disaster so quickly?

Once her legs were steady, Avery pushed off the wall. Squaring her chin, she headed toward the elevator. Inside the compartment, she smiled at the older couple already in there. The pair had their hands clasped, and Avery looked away. Because of the way she protected herself, she might never experience that kind of easy intimacy with a partner.

She exited when the car swished to a stop. Through

willpower, she held her emotions in check while she walked to her room.

Inside, she dropped her clutch on the table, then made her way into the bathroom to take off her mask.

The reflection in the mirror stunned her.

Mascara stained beneath her eyes. Her hair was a wild mess. Worse, her lower lip trembled.

Cole and his opinions didn't matter. They'd shared an evening together, and it meant nothing.

The lie rocked her, making her grip the vanity.

Those hours had been spectacular. She'd achieved the floating sensation that she'd sought for so many years. She'd taken more than she'd imagined she could. He'd given her orgasm after orgasm that left her shattered, not broken, and somehow more complete.

But at what cost?

CHAPTER FIVE

Goddamn it.

He had a reputation as a ladies' man. As such, Cole wasn't known to be a fuckup with the fairer sex. Then again, he'd never been with a woman like Avery Fisher.

When the door had closed behind her, he'd been tempted to ride the elevator to the casino level and drink a few beers at one of the six bars.

Instead, he changed into workout gear. Whether he wanted to or not, he would deal with his emotions head-on, like he demanded from Avery. It was easy to live in denial. But experience had taught him that reality was worth the fight.

He entered the gym, or the Royal Sterling's mind-blowing definition of a gym. Designed by Sean Finnegan, Next Level occupied most of the tenth floor.

Though the aesthetics were stunning, Cole was a simple man. All he needed was a place to run and some significant weights. When he had no other options, his own body could be used for resistance, push-ups, sit-ups, planks.

He bypassed the cardio equipment and went for the free-weight area. Despite it being the middle of the night, the place was busy. Not that it should be a surprise, he supposed. Las Vegas was the planet's playground, and who knew what time zone people were on?

He did squats until his legs burned, curls until his biceps bulged. After a drink of water, he headed for the running track. Maybe the mindless repetition would help him forget the image of Avery's skin turning pink, then red, and her quiet moans of appreciation.

A couple of miles later, a sledgehammer plowed into him. The problem was not her. It was him.

Scening with someone who wanted to keep her identity a secret was fucked-up. And he'd done it anyway. It didn't matter what rationale he used. It had been a bad decision.

But the truth was, he'd have done anything for a night with her.

It had been one hell of an evening. He'd been hot for her curvy, submissive body, and he'd enjoyed every moment they spent together.

If he'd forced her to take off the mask, she might not have had the nerve to scene with him.

The disguise had been the confidence booster she needed and the thing that left him hanging now. He was beyond disappointed that she'd fled instead of trusting him.

He continued to push himself on the track until his lungs begged for a reprieve. And when he began his cooldown, his thoughts were still fragmented.

Honesty was nonnegotiable. And when she was ready, there were a thousand things he intended to do to her, from fucking her ass, to putting her on an iron cross, to scening with her in public, to licking her pussy for so long that the only thing she screamed was his name.

Damn it.

Damn *her.*

On his wrist, his Bonds watch vibrated.

Maybe it was Avery, admitting she'd made a horrible mistake and saying she wanted to be real with him.

Dreamer.

He checked the screen. *Interesting.* A text message from Hawkeye himself.

Go to secure line.

Nothing like work to distract Cole's snarling Dominant beast. *Thank fuck.*

He glanced around to be certain no one was close before selecting the icon for an encrypted line. Then he tapped his earbuds to connect the call.

"Got something interesting."

As usual, Hawkeye didn't indulge in time-wasting pleasantries.

"You interested in taking a trip?"

He slowed to a walk to concentrate on the conversation. "I'm listening."

"We have an appointment in Houston tomorrow. Cristian LaRosa would like to meet you."

What the actual hell?

"He's intrigued by what you've got to offer."

Which was an AI—artificial intelligence—platform unlike anything else on the market. Because Hawkeye protected the world's most valuable people and assets, including secrets, the firm was now Cole's biggest client. But LaRosa? "You busting my balls?" Even as he asked the question, he knew the answer. Hawkeye didn't joke, especially about something like this.

"He's legit."

"Bullshit." Though nothing had ever been proven, the LaRosas were honored as royalty among Mafia families.

"They're planning to open a resort casino here in Vegas, and they have other…business interests stateside and around the world."

Casinos and their resorts were high-profile hacking targets. Which was why he was currently working with Hawkeye on upgrading the Royal Sterling. But working with the mob? That was a line Cole hesitated to cross, despite the fact that Cristian was also a member of the Zeta Society. "Not interested in anything that will raise my profile with the Feds."

"Do your research. Their corporation is completely aboveboard."

Yeah. "Not convinced."

"He's looking at other companies."

"Let him. There's nothing this sophisticated on the market."

"Everyone fucking knows that." Hawkeye's words were clipped with impatience.

Cole wanted to refuse. But a stray image slipped through his brain. One of Avery on her knees looking up at him as she prepared to suck him off. Being in one place for several months was an unheard-of luxury. If he wanted Avery, it gave him some time to plan and execute a strategy.

"I need your answer now, and it needs to be yes," Hawkeye finished.

"Earth to Avery."

She shook her head to clear it then accepted a glass of ginger ale from her friend Makenna. "Thank you."

"Where are you?"

"I'm sorry."

Zara took a sip of her own soft drink, then glanced at Avery. "She's thinking about Cole."

Her friend was right. It had been a week since Avery spent the night with Cole at the Royal Sterling, and she still wanted him. Not just his touch, but his possession.

"There's only one way to get that man out of your head." Makenna scanned the great room of Diana and Alcott Hewitt's astounding home in the John S. Park neighborhood.

For a month, Avery had planned to attend the party, but it had taken every ounce of her energy to change out of the yoga pants she'd worn the entire day. Staying home to watch television was more appealing than interacting with people.

But her friends had texted that they were wondering where she was. Without her customary enthusiasm, she'd wriggled into a tight skirt and bustier. Finally, she donned a bolero jacket so she looked somewhat appropriate for leaving her apartment. With her nose wrinkled, she studied herself in the mirror. The truth was, only one man's opinion of the outfit mattered to her.

Now, she wished she hadn't attended.

"Oh my God. That's Master Zachary…" Makenna fanned herself.

Possessing the fearlessness that came from holding her own against four protective older brothers, Zara grinned. "You should go talk to him."

Makenna shook her head. Though she attended a lot of scene parties, she professed to being far too self-conscious to actually join in. Her favorite spot was in front of the viewing room. "I'll just enjoy watching the demonstrations." She took another sip. Maybe trying to hide her emotions?

"So how about it?" Zara asked Avery "Should we find you a Top to play with?"

Allowing her mind to be consumed with thoughts of a one-night Dominant was ridiculous, but Avery couldn't help herself. "Maybe another time."

For the next hour, they wandered the grounds and observed a few scenes. When a man joined them, with eyes only for Avery, her friends promised to watch out for her, then wandered away together.

He wore leather pants and an unfastened vest that was at least one size too small. Since he'd been invited by the Hewitts, he'd been vetted, which meant he could be trusted. Unfortunately she had zero attraction to him.

"Are you a submissive?"

Unable to find her voice, she settled for nodding.

He swept a glance over her. "Looking for a scene?"

Rather than her heart leaping, disappointment that he wasn't Cole snaked through her. Mentally, she was comparing this man to him. She shook herself. *How screwed up is that?*

Too late, she realized scening with Cole had been a mistake. Everything about him had gotten to her, and she wished it hadn't. He'd ruined her for other men. She was his.

"So, are you?"

Avery blinked herself back to the present. "No. I'm not." Then she smiled to take the sting from the rejection. "Thank you, though."

She wandered into the great room where a woman was dressed in office attire—a tight white shirt, a short skirt, black pumps, and stockings. A man wearing a business suit instructed her to bend over the desk.

Restlessness momentarily abated, Avery watched.

The Dom worked the woman's skirt up, exposing her scantily clad bottom, with the straps on her garter belt bisecting her butt cheeks. Then he shrugged out of his jacket. "What have I told you about surfing social media during work hours?" He picked up a cane.

The sub looked over her shoulder, her mouth open wide with pretend fear. Or maybe the reaction was real. Avery would never be able to face the cane with anything less than complete respect.

"Oh, Mr. Holmes! I promise I won't ever do that again. Please spare me!"

"How many times have you been warned? Hmm? Two? Three? You knew there would be consequences."

Those words echoed in Avery's head. She should have thought through the consequences of scening with Master Cole.

He'd told her he would spoil her for any other man. And he had. But she hadn't been prepared for being adrift without him.

The Dom gathered the material of his sub's panties and moved it all to her crotch, then yanked, lifting her from the floor.

Avery winced in mute sympathy as the Dominant smacked the woman's bare buttocks before letting loose with the cane.

The sound, the way the woman flinched, then the terrible thin line on her skin, brought it all back for Avery.

She yearned for Cole, wanted to be naked, sobbing beneath his dominance. She craved the orgasm he would give her.

The Dom delivered another stroke.

The truth crept up on Avery and hit her as powerfully as a stripe from rattan. It was the connection—emotional as well as physical—that she thirsted for. Cole had held her, caressed her. He'd cared for her, making her feel special. His loving attention had boosted her confidence.

With a hole in her heart, she wandered outside where a couple was demonstrating rope bondage. Watching the slow beauty and intricacies of Shibari often relaxed her. Tonight it made her lonely.

She should have trusted her earlier instincts. Coming here had been a mistake.

Once she accepted that, she found her friends and said her goodbyes.

Avery took her time driving home, avoiding the congestion of the Strip. But it wasn't just the overwhelming traffic that kept her away. It was the realization she would end up at the Royal Sterling, looking for Cole.

And she didn't have it in her to agree to his ultimatum.

She stopped at a traffic light and dropped her head onto the steering wheel.

Why the hell am I making this so complicated?

No doubt, what he had demanded of her would be difficult. She was accustomed to letting her man—her Dom—be in charge. And Dirk's scoldings had been a constant narrative during a scene.

Beneath the mask, she'd become someone different, but what if she could learn to be that person all the time?

The car behind her honked impatiently, alerting her to the fact that the light had turned green. She accelerated, and so did her thoughts and heart rate.

She'd gained confidence from her time with Master Cole. What if he encouraged and supported her growth?

He'd been right when he'd told her she needed to be honest with herself. So she allowed herself to admit she wanted, needed him.

Now what?

It would take a ton of resolve to act on her newfound admission, to either show up at his hotel room or ask Diana for his number.

Unfortunately, Avery wasn't that brave, no matter how much she wanted to be.

Avery spent Sunday doing chores and working out. When she returned home, she tried a couple of different books. When neither held her, she settled in front of the television and binged her way through an entire season of a home improvement show. To prove to herself that she wasn't hopeless, she opened a bottle of expensive special-occasion wine, then poured herself a glass.

It didn't help.

No matter what she did, she couldn't escape the fact that her cowardice was the major contributor to her unhappiness.

Once she was in her bedroom, she slipped the bullet vibrator inside her pussy and masturbated to memories of Cole. They were a thousand times more potent than her imagination ever had been.

Even more frustrating, she was unable to climax.

Annoyed, she removed the toy, cleaned it, then dropped it back into her drawer.

At work on Monday morning, two of Avery's coworkers followed her into the break room to chat about their weekend outings, the movies they'd seen, the parties they'd attended. When asked about her time off, she replied noncommittally, then went into her office and got busy on her spreadsheets behind a closed door.

She stayed later than most people, and at six o'clock, Aunt Scarlet dropped by her office.

"Darling girl." Her great-aunt took plopped into a seat without waiting for an invitation. "You didn't return my call."

Since her aunt was too perceptive at times, Avery had dodged the two Sunday calls. She should have expected Scarlet to show up in person.

"It's a man, isn't it?"

"I'm sorry?"

"When you hide from me, it's because of a man."

"I wasn't hiding."

Aunt Scarlet's eyes went wide, sending her lashes soaring. "You were hiding."

"Okay." Avery sank a little lower in her chair. "Maybe I was."

"Tell me about him."

"You seem to have done quite well without a man."

"That's because I had dozens. Still do. I like"—she waved a ring-covered hand—"variety, shall we say. I like rich ones and creatives ones. Skilled lovers. Men who will jet me to their island. Mostly, I like my independence. It's cost me some relationships." She took a breath, and she blinked rapidly. It couldn't be tears, could it? "Some I regret."

The moisture in her aunt's eyes vanished so fast that Avery was sure she'd imagined it. "Do you?"

"Yes. Not many. But I do wonder about Billy."

The mobster? "What would you do differently?"

"Nothing. I have to live with some scars, but to me, it's worth it. You, however, are different. Such a tender heart."

"So what do you recommend I do?"

"Oh, heavens! I would never give you advice!"

"But if you did?"

"Live with no regrets. Do what makes you happy. Anything can be undone. Except, perhaps, chances you didn't take."

Avery exhaled.

"It's the delicious secret agent man, isn't it?" Aunt Scarlet leaned forward, as if soliciting a secret. "Cole."

"Yes."

"Oh, honey. The way he looked at you." She shimmied, and in the process moved forward a couple of inches in her chair. "He wants you."

"He gave me an ultimatum."

"Ah," she replied, as if she understood. "A man who knows what he wants. He's good to you?"

He was.

"And you wouldn't be suffering if you didn't care for him."

Avery exhaled.

"So, if I were to give advice, which I don't, I'd say give it a try. Well, unless the terms of his ultimatum are dreadful. Are they?"

"Emotionally, maybe."

"It's up to you, then. If the risk isn't worth the reward, spend the next six months moping."

Offended, she responded. "I'm not moping."

"You are. And that's not living. So, forget him and go have some fun tonight. See a movie. Try a new restaurant. Or be brave and see where it goes. If it doesn't work out, at least you'll know. You might get hurt, but you won't have the scars of never knowing and always wondering what might have been."

"When did you get to be so wise?"

"I was born this way. And so were you." She winked. "Chin up, darling girl." Aunt Scarlet grabbed the handle of her oversize purse. Rising, she said, "If you'll excuse me, Gerard is in town. And this is an evening I fully intend to embrace. No show tonight. Well…except for his command performance."

"Wait." Avery blinked. "Gerard who?"

"He was in a few movies or…something on television. He looks good in a kilt. Very nice legs."

"You've got to tell me," Avery demanded.

Scarlet rounded the desk to drop a kiss on Avery's forehead. "Remember to choose the path that will help you live with no regrets." Without another word, Aunt Scarlet breezed out, letting her wisdom linger on a cloud of perfume.

Avery collapsed against the back of her seat. For several minutes, the conversation replayed in her mind.

Walking away from Cole had left a hole deep inside. She could go on with her life, but one point that Scarlet made continued to resonate. If she agreed to Cole's terms, Avery might very well get hurt, but she wouldn't have to live with not knowing how it might have turned out.

Contemplatively, she tapped a finger on the arm of her chair.

Could she do it? Take the chance?

It would mean being honest. Not just with him, but with herself.

She blew out a breath to steady her nerves. The truth was, if she didn't at least try, she would be disappointed in herself. She needed to be as brave without a mask as she had been wearing one.

Before her newfound resolve fled, she picked up her phone to text Diana for Cole's number.

It didn't mean Avery had to contact him. It just meant she could, if she decided to.

Instead of staring at the phone, waiting for a response that might not come, she dropped the device into her purse, then straightened her desk before leaving for the night.

Her phone chimed while she was navigating traffic, so she waited until she was at a stoplight to check her messages.

Diana had replied in her customary precise way. She'd

attached Cole's contact card, with all his information—email address, social media accounts, and his cell phone. His number showed up in blue, which meant all Avery just had to do was touch the screen to be connected.

She moved her finger toward the number and hovered over it.

But she couldn't make herself tap the number. Thank God, the light turned green, allowing her to put off the action a little longer.

By the time she arrived home, nerves were pouring through her. She was going to call him. But then what would she do if he didn't answer? Leave a message? What would she say? What if he didn't call back? Her mind skipped through a dozen different scenarios before she harnessed her thoughts and took a breath, drawing on the coaching he'd given her when they scened.

She made herself face the fact that he might reject her. If so, at least she would know. She'd be no more hurt than she was right now.

But if he wanted to see her…

That possibility made her tighten her grip.

By the time she arrived home, she'd made her decision.

She walked down the hallway leading to her apartment, and her step faltered. A man stood near her door. Not just any man—one who was tall, broad, unshaven, sexy. He wore a charcoal-gray suit, and his only concession to it being after work hours was the loosened knot in his tie. Stunned, she stopped near him. "Master Cole."

"Avery." He pushed away from the wall.

"You know who I am." *Of course.* He had all of Hawkeye's resources at his fingertips.

"I've known all along."

Nervously she tucked her hair behind her ears. "There's no way."

"I saw you, that night when I was at Alcott and Diana's with Gia. I overheard your friends calling you Avery, and the name was unusual, beautiful, so I remembered it. It could have been a scene name," he allowed. "But I didn't get the sense it was. Then I noticed you at the club about six months ago."

"Those sleuthing skills come in handy."

"I was hoping you'd be brave enough to come to me. Or hell... I was so intrigued by you that I would have made a move if you'd shown enough interest."

She lurched, as if the world had suddenly started to spin backward.

"Your eyes, Avery. They give away the world. The way you walk, your ass swaying? Your body is so damn sexy. Hair length, color? Mask?" He shrugged. "It wouldn't matter how you altered your appearance. I would always know you."

Damn, he'd told her he could be counted on to give her what she needed. He left her speechless.

"Since you contacted Diana, I wanted to meet you halfway. I would never ask you to take all the risk. I do want you to ask for what you want, but I will make it easy for you. You will always know I respect and value you. I brought you a cupcake in case I need to bribe my way inside." From behind his back, he presented a gorgeous pink box wrapped with a white ribbon. "It's triple chocolate."

"You're an evil man." But oh, so wonderfully sweet.

"I'm holding it hostage."

It might have been her imagination, but she swore she could smell the sugar in the frosting.

"I was going to give you another couple of days; then I'd have been all over you. I've been crazy with missing you. If you refused to see me, I planned to hang out near the cupcake machine, figuring you'd show up eventually."

A neighbor and her two boys who were punching each

other entered the hallway.

Avery moved her keys from hand to hand. "I think you should come in."

Seconds later, he locked the door behind them, and she hung her purse from the coatrack.

In the kitchen, he placed her gift on the counter.

"I missed you too." Her words were soft. "Terribly." This was difficult, but the longer she talked, the easier it got. "Being honest with you has to be easier than not being with you."

"That night, before you left, you said there were costs to everything. Asking for too much. *Being* too much. Tell me about it."

Her first test. "Can we, uhm…? How about something to drink?"

"No. I'm fine. But you can, if you wish."

She shook her head. "But I would like us to sit in the living room."

He followed, and she perched on the edge of an armchair, while he lowered himself onto the sofa. He leaned forward and laced his fingers on top of his knees.

"I've been single for over a year." Avery drew a breath. She hadn't shared these details with anyone. Cole remained silent, waiting while she collected her thoughts. "My boyfriend—Dominant—said I wanted to scene too often." She paused. That wasn't quite the truth. His wording had hurt more. "He was supposed to be in charge, so that meant everything in our relationship was up to him." With a little shrug, she went on. "I stopped asking. I accepted what little he offered, and I was grateful for it. I was…but at the same time, I wasn't. I began to think he was right. Maybe my sex drive was too high. I was restless, feeling neglected. We played once a month, if that. I made the mistake of asking if we could go to Diana and Alcott's one night, and Dirk

83

snapped." After a breath, she confessed the shame. "He called me an ungrateful bitch. Then he left. I never heard from him again."

"Jesus, Avery. I had no idea."

"That night, behind the mask, I could be the woman I wanted to be. I needed that crutch to shut out his voice in my head. It was my first scene in a really long time."

He dragged the knot from his tie. "What he told you was bullshit. You're exquisite in every way."

She gave a ghost of a smile as relief poured through her. "It's going to take me some time. But if you have the patience, I want to try."

"Will you come to me?" He extended his hand.

On shaky legs, she stood.

She crossed the room to him; then he eased her into his lap, facing him with her knees on the cushions. His eyes were melted steel, offering promise and reassurance. "You're enough. We will figure this out together."

Drinking in his approval, she nodded.

"Tell me what you want."

"I want you to kiss me, Sir. I want to wrap my arms around your neck. I want you to be hard with me. I like it rough. I want you to put your leg between mine so I can rub my hot pussy on you. I'm desperate to come. I've been masturbating, but I haven't been able to have an orgasm. And if you tell me I can't have all of those things—any of those things—I will say yes, Sir, and be happy. Just be my Dom."

He put his hands on either side of her head and kissed her, long, slow, stoking embers until the flames roared into an inferno. She inhaled his spice and the freshness of honesty. His breath was warm on her face, and he moved his thigh between hers, achingly close to her pussy.

"Are you horny for me?" His eyes narrowed, and she shuddered.

"Yes. As always."

"I want you, Avery. First, you need to be rewarded for your honesty. Lift up your skirt."

Because it was so tight, it took her a few seconds to do as he instructed.

"Ah. Panties. Just like the night at the Royal Sterling. I guessed you were the type of woman who would wear them unless your Dom instructed otherwise."

She met his eyes.

"Consider yourself instructed."

She shivered. "Yes, Sir."

"Get rid of them."

Since that was a difficult task in her position, he helped her.

"Now put your arms around my neck." He dampened his finger, then glided it across her clit.

His touch was exquisite. She wrapped her arms around him and moved in rhythm with his strokes. There was no place she would rather be.

"I want you to be thinking…"

"Sir?"

"About how many stripes you're going to get from my cane."

Fear, excitement, doubt, hope all surged through her. "You don't have it."

"In the car, I do," he countered. "I'm thinking three for each day you've been gone."

"That's too many," she protested, scared, hungry.

"Better idea?"

"No, Sir."

"Let's go get my cane."

In that moment, she knew—*knew*—he would give her what she needed. She sighed, content, maybe for the first time ever.

EPILOGUE

"So..." Avery reached for her Dom's tie and began to loosen the knot at his throat. Four months prior, she'd moved in to Cole's beautiful house. Built on more than half an acre on a cul-de-sac up against a mountain in a gated community, it was as much a fortress as it was a place to retreat. The fenced perimeter was protected by a state-of-the-art security system designed by Cole himself and tweaked by the tech genius, Julien Bonds.

Anyone approaching the fence was greeted by a rather polite British voice advising that they were trespassing and that the police had been notified. In addition, video was livestreamed to the authorities. There were other fences and tripwires, and, of course, the house itself had a secure room with numerous monitors that also could be accessed from Cole's cell phone.

A little at a time, he'd shared some stories from his past, and she understood his need to know what was coming before it arrived. To his credit, though, he'd realized she needed more comfort than he did. They spent most of their weekends working together to transform the six thousand square feet into a home. She'd set up a place to work, and the previous day, he'd surprised her by having several potted palms delivered for their living room.

They'd spent considerable time discussing their relationship and expectations. He had cut back his travel schedule, and when he returned to her, he always pulled her tight and kept her there.

"So...?" he prompted.

She took a breath. Each time she stated her needs, it was easier. But it was still far from natural, even though he was true to his promise and made it as easy as possible for her. "Diana and Alcott are having a play party next weekend."

"Are they?"

Avery tugged the knot open and left the ends of the bloodred tie hanging down his jacket. She couldn't get enough of him. Every day he assured her it was more than mutual. "I'd like to go, Sir."

A slow smile crossed his face. "Would you?"

"I ordered a new outfit. Just in case you said yes."

He lifted one eyebrow in a sexy way that showed his interest and shot heat through her. That was something she adored about him. When they were together, all of his attention was devoted to her. Many nights they took a dip—naked—in the pool. Sometimes they curled up on their new couch and watched her favorite drama. At least twice a week, he spent considerable time planning a scene that shattered her, healed her. "Tell me about the new clothes."

"The top is called a bralette. But it's a little more complicated than that."

"Lace?"

"Leather, and it sort of looks like a harness."

"That may be my new favorite word." He pulled her against him. "I'm thrilled to have people see you wearing it."

He touched her collarbone. "And of course, I will want to attach a leash to it when we attend the party."

His cock was raging hard, and she guessed what was next. Still, she waited on the command she knew was coming.

"Drop your clothes, Avery." His words were forged in steel, instantly dropping her into a submissive state of mind. Cole knew her sensual triggers, and his voice was the most powerful.

He released his grip on her. In a fluid movement, she pulled her sundress up and off, then dropped it to the floor before kicking off her sandals.

He swept his approving gaze over her. "Let me see you."

She drew a steadying breath, no longer from concern. He appreciated *her*, everything about her, even the things she considered flaws.

Avery turned her back to him, spread her legs as wide as possible, then held her ankles.

"So gorgeous." He grabbed her ass cheeks and squeezed. Hard.

His fingers dug deep enough to hurt, but she didn't wince. Instead, she closed her eyes in submission.

"All day, I thought about this," he said, spreading her wide for his inspection. He skimmed his finger across her private parts, being sure she'd complied with this morning's order to be clean-shaven.

Not knowing what to expect was an extra bonus. At times, he wanted her natural. Once he'd directed her to be neatly trimmed. Mostly, he wanted her bare. He didn't allow her to anticipate and in fact had chastised her for doing so. Since it had hurt to sit down after that, she'd learned her lesson.

He was the Dom—in charge—in the best way possible. Over their months together, she'd learned to trust him. He didn't criticize her or have mercurial moods. They'd had a few disagreements, but they'd sat together at the dining table, across from each other, taking turns talking, with no raised voices.

Over time, trust had blossomed into the first tendrils of love. She'd passed infatuation, and the more powerful emotion was new and a little scary, leaving her giddy.

"How long since you've tasted my belt?"

Her world swam.

"Answer me." His words were soft, but his tone was not.

She thought back. His cane, she remembered. And his hand. Even the flogger. "Too long, Sir."

"I agree. Let's rectify that." He released her. "I want you over the back of the couch."

Conscious of him watching her every move, she brought herself upright and walked across the room to get into the position he'd requested.

Cole said nothing, allowing the time to drag and her tension to build.

Something crinkled, and she turned her head to the side to see what he was doing, but he wasn't in her range of sight. She could guess what he was doing—removing his suit coat? And his tie? Rolling up his shirtsleeves?

Her breath whooshed out when he lifted her, tipping her forward. Frantic, she grabbed for a cushion for stability. "Sir!"

"Much better. Don't you agree?"

Her feet no longer touched the stone floor, but she knew better than to argue. "Yes, Cole." Something cold and wet pressed against her rear. She froze.

"Clenching will make it worse, Avery."

Breathing deep in this position was almost impossible—especially with him doing evil things to her.

He pressed forward. Avery's tightest hole stretched to

accommodate him, as it always did. "Urgh." The metal snuggled in.

"Very nice." Cole twisted the plug around and around, driving her out of her mind. "I love having your ass stuffed full."

Because it heightened her arousal and because it pleased him, she liked it too.

To warm her up, he smoothed his hands over her back and shoulders, then her buttocks, even the tops of her thighs. She allowed her body to go limp, going to a place deep inside her mind where she could push away the stresses of the world and connect with her Dom.

The first few strokes of his belt were soft, a hint of what was to come. As the minutes drew on, he deepened the intensity.

"Leather was made for your ass."

"Yes." The word emerged as a mumble, but he understood, as he always did.

The next stripe caught her beneath the buttocks. She yelped from the wave of pain. Within seconds, it eased off, and pleasure surged in.

He slid his finger between her labia. "You like this."

Avery struggled to stay in place, but she was so aroused that she jutted herself backward, seeking more.

He laughed, a diabolical sound, and moved his finger away from her.

Protesting would earn her a longer spanking, so she clamped her lips together.

"You are a quick study." Approval laced his words, making her glad she'd remained quiet.

He gave her ten more stripes, each one making her cry out louder. And when it was over, he helped her up.

Overwhelmed, she slipped to her knees.

Shocking her, he knelt too, facing her. He took her hands

in his, and she met his eyes. For once, they were unreadable, their gray color lighter than normal, like liquid silver.

"Sir?"

"I love you, Avery."

His words and the pure conviction in them made her shake. A lump lodged in her throat, making it impossible to respond.

"I've known it for a long time, but I didn't think you were ready to trust the words, until now." He continued to hold her with one hand, and he used the other to notch her chin up. His smile was tentative, and it was one of the few times she'd caught a glimpse of him without his customary alpha male confidence. It humbled her, revealed the depth of his honesty. "It's okay if you don't return the sentiment—"

"I..." Desperately trying to swallow the wedge of emotion, she nodded. The tears spilled.

With exquisite tenderness, he used his thumb to capture one, but he didn't try to wipe them away. "I'm taking it that means you love me too?"

The words, admission, came from deep inside her. "Oh Cole..."

He kissed her intimately, with domination, but also with affection. She clung to him and his strength as if she never wanted to let go. He tasted of promise. Of a hundred thousand tomorrows.

When neither of them could breathe anymore, he ended the kiss.

"That was..." She managed to dislodge the knot in her throat. "I love you, Cole. There's never been anyone like you in my life."

"Precious, precious sub." He grinned, a cocky tilt to his mouth. The macho Dom was once again in control. "We should order some food. You've got a long night ahead of you, and you're not leaving the house for a very long time.

Now that I have you naked and plugged, I plan to keep you that way."

Oh. "For how long?"

"The rest of your life will do." His eyes gleamed. "For a start."

◊ ◊ ◊ ◊ ◊

Thank you for reading Hard Hand. I hope you enjoyed Cole and Avery's story. I enjoy masked balls, and some of the Mardi Gras events here in Galveston gave me inspiration for this story. Pretending to be someone else for a night can be lots of fun, and in this case, the anonymity gave Avery a chance to be braver than she usually is. Of course, Cole wasn't falling for it. And I loved that about him.

Las Vegas is an intriguing place, and it's an ideal setting for Titans, the world's richest, most powerful alphas.

The Sin City world continues with Slow Burn featuring hero Zachary Denning, a former military Dom who is as exacting as he is relentless.

DISCOVER SLOW BURN

Have you met the delicious, ultra-sexy heroes of the Quarter in New Orleans? She only agreed to a weekend together. Now the overwhelming billionaire Dominant is demanding Hannah's heart forever.

★ ★ ★ ★ ★ Full of real, raw, beautiful emotions with vibrant characters. ~Amazon Reviewer

DISCOVER HIS TO CLAIM

Turn the page for an exciting excerpt from SLOW BURN

SLOW BURN

CHAPTER ONE

"What do you see?"

Makenna jumped, sending diet soda over the rim of her glass to splash on the polished hardwood floor. The question, unexpected, soft, sexy, gruff, and growly against her ear, rocketed sparks of desire down her spine.

Although they'd never been introduced, she'd recognize his commanding baritone anywhere. For years, Zachary Denning had starred in her dreams and strolled through her fantasies.

The renowned Dominant was ridiculously rich, movie-star handsome, a battlefield hero...and a notorious heartbreaker. Master Zachary could have any woman on the planet, and from what she'd witnessed—tonight even—there was always a line clamoring for his attention.

So why was he talking to her?

"I didn't mean to startle you."

She started to turn, but he clamped his strong hands on her shoulders, igniting a firestorm inside her.

"No. Please. Stay where you are."

Her pulse skittered, and her breath caught in her throat.

There was no way he could know the intoxicating effect he had on her.

"That scene has you fascinated."

Since she was momentarily speechless, she settled for nodding.

Every few months, she and her friends from a women-in-business group attended a play party here at the home of Las Vegas's hottest legal eagles, Diana and Alcott Hewitt.

Not only were the couple partners at the law firm bearing their name, but they owned one of the city's most unique properties, a house that was over twenty thousand square feet with grounds that sprawled over three large lots. The U-shaped home had an amazing courtyard complete with lush tropical foliage and swimming pool with attached hot tub. Farther out was a dramatic and rather noisy waterfall. And for clandestine meetings, a grotto was tucked away in the darkest recesses of the garden.

This evening, Makenna stood in front of her favorite place, an observation room, complete with one-way glass. The hot BDSM scene transpiring between her hosts had her riveted. That was the only explanation possible for not noticing Master Zachary's arrival.

"Tell me what you see." It was his second prompt, and command laced his request, compelling an obedience she'd never before explored.

Unnerved by the billionaire as much as her own response to him, she cleared her throat. "I was about to move on."

"Were you?" His tone was warm, with an underlying mocking note. He'd caught her in a lie and called it out.

Impossibly, then, he moved in closer. She imagined the abrasive rub of his pants against the bare skin of her legs.

Master Zachary had a reputation as a considerate Dominant, which meant she could excuse herself and make an escape at any time. Maybe that's why she remained rooted in place.

"You want to watch every moment until the very end." He slid the words into her ear, his breath warm on her already heated skin. "That's why you're here, isn't it?"

In a rush, she exhaled the painful admission. "Yes."

On the other side of the glass, Master Alcott held up a palm. Diana, naked and collared, sank to her knees and lowered her head. Then, in a move both beautiful and practiced, she cupped her breasts, then offered them—and herself—to her Dominant.

"Is that what you want? To be in that position?"

Frantically Makenna shook her head. "I'm not much of a submissive." But if she were, it would be with Master Zachary. He didn't need a set of weights. He was simply blessed by the gods with a body that wouldn't quit.

"You're not much of a submissive?" Disbelief roughened his question. "You haven't moved from this place for at least ten minutes."

Which meant he'd been watching her. Had he noticed the way she squirmed when Master Alcott had stripped his wife? "Ah…I find it interesting." She cleared her throat. "A curiosity."

"Are you aroused?"

"What?" Heat rushed through her. She was glad he couldn't see the way excitement vanquished her shock.

"Is your pussy wet?"

Oh my God. Embarrassment clogged her throat.

"Be brave."

She couldn't.

"Take a chance. For me."

Because his order was as compelling as it was nonnegotiable, she nodded.

"I'd like to hear the words."

"Yes." Could she do this? Could she not? "I'm wet."

"That pleases me immensely. Yet you hesitated. What are you afraid of?"

"I'm an event planner. I deal with brides and demanding C-types all day long. Nothing scares me." She tried for an air of lightness she didn't feel.

"There are things in this world that are absolutely terrifying."

Of course he would know. She'd read an article in her favorite gossip magazine, *Scandalicious,* about his exploits. Though he was from a wealthy background, all the Denning men were expected to serve their country. He'd graduated from a military academy and served heroically in battle before joining the family business. How they made their money, she had no idea. But she'd heard plenty of whispers.

He eased closer, rocketing response through her and forcing her to admit she was afraid of something. *Him.*

In front of them, Master Alcott took a bit gag down from the wall. His beautiful wife continued to stare at him and, without being told, opened her mouth. He placed the gag between her teeth, checked it for fit, then buckled the strap tightly behind her head.

At the sight of Diana's compliance, a bizarre buzzing scrambled around in Makenna's ears.

"Describe the scene to me."

Like a moment ago, his command was absolute. Zachary Denning was a man accustomed to being obeyed. The problem was, until now, even though she had her private daydreams, she wasn't a woman accustomed to being told what to do.

"I'm waiting."

This surreal experience was giving her the opportunity to live out her fantasies, if only for the moment. Despite a rush of nervousness, she spoke. "Master Alcott is helping Diana to stand." Makenna tightened her fingers around her glass. "Now she's walking to the center of the room where there's a massage type of table."

"Keep going."

Is this really happening? "She's bending at the waist, and he's securing her wrists to the far end of the table."

"So she can't move?"

Makenna squirmed. "Not much."

"So theoretically Master Alcott can do whatever he wants to her?"

A shiver rippled through her. "Yes."

"And since she's gagged, she can't say anything. She can't beg for mercy or protest in any way."

Words failed Makenna.

"Do you wonder what it might be like to be in there? To be completely helpless to your Dominant's whims? To have others watching you?"

Her mouth dried. She took a sip of the soda, trying to ignore the fact her hand was shaking. "Of course not. I've already told you I'm not submissive."

His soft chuckle was more of a scoff. "And your reactions tell a different story. Your breathing." He stroked a finger down the side of her throat. "The fluttering here." He pressed a thumb against her pulse.

If he hadn't kept one hand clamped on her shoulder, she would have fled.

"You haven't told me to go to hell."

Because foolishly she wanted this.

"Let me take your drink, Makenna."

Her pulse skipped a beat, then slammed the next dozen together. "How do you know who I am?" Maybe she should have selected a scene name to hide her identity, though she suspected he would dig through as many layers as it took to discover the information he wanted.

"I make it my business to know all of Diana and Alcott's guests, particularly the beautiful ones."

Beautiful? Not at all, and especially not when compared to the women he was known to date. Despite eating more lettuce than a rabbit, skipping chocolate for long enough to bankrupt Switzerland, and sweating at the gym three times a week, she had bulges and ripples everywhere. "I'm afraid you have the wrong person."

"Be assured, I don't."

What game are you playing?

With strength that gave her no chance to run, he turned her to face him. For a moment, he stroked her shoulders, so sensually that her insides began to unravel. Then, when he tightened his fingers again, she tipped back her head to meet his gaze.

This close, he made her tremble.

He wore black jeans rather than leather pants. A T-shirt hugged his upper body, emphasizing the cut and definition of his well-honed biceps. Scuffed motorcycle boots added an inch or two to his height, not that he needed it. He was already over six feet tall, towering over her, even in her heels.

But it was his eyes that riveted her attention. They were dark and deep, like the Atlantic during a tumultuous storm. His strong jaw was set in a firm line. No matter how hard she tried, she couldn't bear to look away from the intensity blazing in his expression.

At that moment, a male server wearing tight black trousers and a red bowtie approached.

Master Zachary finally released her to take her glass. After placing it on the tray, he snagged a napkin to wipe up her earlier spill.

His thoughtfulness surprised her.

When they were alone again, he took a slight step back and swept his gaze over her. If what her ex-boyfriend said was true, Master Zachary was cataloging her numerous flaws.

"Gorgeous. Simply gorgeous."

She blinked at his reaction.

"Now, I'd like your legs shoulder width apart."

She had no idea what he had in mind, but if she offered him the control he wanted, she would never again be the same.

"You're hesitating. And again, you haven't told me to go to hell."

Master Zachary's presence was as undeniable as it was compelling.

"Courage, Makenna. Why not seize the moment?"

With a shaky breath, she did as he instructed, terribly aware of how short her skirt was.

"You follow directions well. You please me."

His approval weakened her knees. It had been so, so long...

"Now face the scene again."

As before, he placed his hands on her shoulders, but this time, his grip was possessive.

While they watched, Master Alcott slid his hand between Diana's legs. The woman arched her back, as if silently asking for more.

"Please continue your narration."

"Master Alcott seems to be stroking Diana's..." Makenna trailed off. "Her clit."

"And does she seem to be enjoying it?"

"Yes." As much as possible, Diana lifted her body, seemingly begging for her Master's touch. Makenna couldn't help but picture herself in Diana's place, with Zachary's strong fingers parting her labia.

Master Alcott moved away. Diana's hips swayed side to side gently and invitingly.

"What is Alcott doing?" Master Zachary asked.

"Ah…" Her eyes widened. "He's getting… Oh my God." Little points of metal winked in the overhead lights. "Vampire gloves."

"Have you ever used them?"

She shook her head. Then she revealed more than she intended. "I haven't experienced most things related to BDSM." Truth was, while she yearned for more, she lacked the courage.

"And are you curious?"

"About the gloves in particular?" She shivered as Master Alcott checked the fit and flexed his fingers. "No. They terrify me."

"I can understand that. Yet the simultaneous dance of pain and pleasure can be addictive."

The image of Master Zachary exploring her body sashayed through her mind.

Intently focused, Master Alcott traced the little spikes up the outsides of his wife's thighs, then the insides, forcing her to rise onto her toes.

Diana turned her head to the side, so Makenna could read her expression. As the Dominant neared his submissive's pussy, she closed her eyes.

Instead of touching her most intimate place, he grabbed hold of her buttocks and squeezed.

Makenna yelped.

Master Zachary chuckled. "Sympathy reaction?"

"That had to hurt."

"Most likely."

Master Alcott said something inaudible before uncurling his fingers to spank the tops of Diana's thighs. Though Makenna winced, the submissive wore a soft smile.

"He knows what she likes and ensures she receives it."

When Master Alcott again traced his way up the insides

of her thighs, Diana parted her legs as far as her restraints allowed, giving herself over to her Dominant. She didn't pull away when he reached her apex.

"Notice the way he's taking in every one of her responses."

To Makenna this was about far more than BDSM. Submitting would mean she trusted a man to keep her best interests at the forefront, something she'd never experienced.

Master Zachary drew Makenna back a step, into a tiny alcove. Willingly, she went.

"I smell your arousal." His statement was a silken scandal, unraveling her resistance. "For what I have in mind, we need a little more privacy."

Run.

As Makenna watched breathlessly, Diana lifted her chest a little, enough for Master Alcott to slide his hands beneath her breasts.

"Accompany me to the grotto."

Unable to think or respond, Makenna froze.

"I promise you a night you will always remember."

She couldn't. Wouldn't. "I'm not your type, Master Zachary."

"On the contrary. You absolutely are." He brushed her hair aside. "Beautiful." Then he placed a gentle kiss on the side of her neck. "Curvy."

That was a kind word, unlike the one her ex had used to describe her.

"Inexperienced yet interested."

Maybe the fact that she hadn't fawned all over him was the appeal. But to her, this was no game. "And you want to be the one to corrupt me?"

"In every way I can think of. And ruin you for every other man."

She shivered. "That's quite…egotistical."

"Not in the least."

In the observation room, Master Alcott removed his gloves, then masturbated his wife while spanking her with his free hand.

Bucking and whimpering, Diana arched toward her Dominant, asking for more. Seconds later, she quivered before collapsing with a gentle shudder.

Master Alcott faced the glass and smiled, then pressed a button to close the blinds, effectively ending the scene. There was no longer any reason for Master Zachary to stay with her.

If Makenna didn't seize this moment, would it ever happen again? Her innate sense of preservation warred with her desire to give herself over to the moment.

"What do you say, my innocent? Are you brave enough to turn yourself over to me for the next hour?"

ABOUT THE AUTHOR

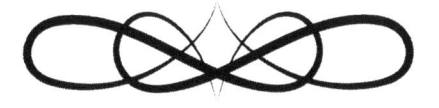

I invite you to be the very first to know all the news by subscribing to my very special **VIP Reader newsletter**! You'll find exclusive excerpts, bonus reads, and insider information.

For tons of fun and to join with other awesome people like you, join my Facebook reader group: **Sierra's Super Stars**

International bestselling author Sierra Cartwright was born in England, and she spent her early childhood traipsing through castles and dreaming of happily-ever afters. She was raised in Colorado and now calls Galveston, Texas home. She loves to connect with her readers, so please feel free to drop her a note.

ALSO BY SIERRA CARTWRIGHT

Titans

Sexiest Billionaire

Billionaire's Matchmaker

Billionaire's Christmas

Determined Billionaire

Scandalous Billionaire

Relentless Billionaire

Titans Quarter

His to Claim

His to Love

His to Cherish

Titans Sin City

Hard Hand

Slow Burn

All-In

Hawkeye

Come to Me

Trust in Me

Meant For Me

Hold On To Me

Believe in Me

Bonds

Crave

Claim

Donovan Dynasty

Bind

Brand

Boss

Mastered

With This Collar

On His Terms

Over The Line

In His Cuffs

For The Sub

In The Den

Collections

Titans Series

Titans Billionaires: Firsts

Titans Billionaires: Volume 1

Hawkeye Series

Here for Me: Volume One

Printed in Great Britain
by Amazon